"Marry me."

Sage didn't react, and TJ wasn't sure if she'd heard the words.

He continued talking. "Share my life, my whole life."

She started to laugh. Her hand rose to her mouth, and she kept laughing.

He was vaguely insulted. "How is that funny?"

"It's not funny." She removed her hand and schooled her features, swallowing. "It's preposterous."

He'd admit it was unorthodox. "It's logical. We share a son."

"We barely know each other."

"A marriage of convenience, obviously." As he said the words, he pictured her in his bed. The vision startled him. He shook it away and pressed on. "Look at the size of this place. We can stay completely out of each other's way. You and Eli can have the entire upstairs to yourselves."

"Take me home, TJ." She looked fragile and forlorn.

She also looked beautiful, and he wanted to draw her into his arms and comfort her. He wanted to hold her, and he wanted to kiss her.

* * *

His Temptation, Her Secret is part of the Whiskey Bay Brides trilogy: Three friends find love on the shores of Whiskey Bay

Dear Reader,

Welcome to the final book in the Whiskey Bay Brides series! The Pacific Northwest was a major inspiration for this series. Between the deep blue ocean, the soaring coastal mountains, the endless islands and the laid-back atmosphere, it's an amazing place to live or to visit.

In *His Temptation, Her Secret*, widower TJ Bauer is confronted by his biggest regret, a woman he'd done wrong in high school. He's astonished to discover Sage Costas is the mother of his son—a son he never knew he had who is in need of a bone marrow transplant.

But saving his son's life is only the beginning. Both Sage and Eli need his support. And whether they like it or not, he's never walking out on them again.

Barbara

BARBARA DUNLOP

———

HIS TEMPTATION, HER SECRET

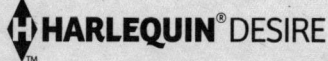

Recycling programs
for this product may
not exist in your area.

ISBN-13: 978-1-335-97133-3

His Temptation, Her Secret

Copyright © 2018 by Barbara Dunlop

Printed in U.S.A.

www.Harlequin.com

New York Times and *USA TODAY* bestselling author **Barbara Dunlop** has written more than forty novels for Harlequin, including the acclaimed Chicago Sons series for Harlequin Desire. Her sexy, lighthearted stories regularly hit bestseller lists. Barbara is a three-time finalist for the Romance Writers of America's RITA® Award.

Books by Barbara Dunlop

Harlequin Desire

Chicago Sons

Sex, Lies and the CEO
Seduced by the CEO
A Bargain with the Boss
His Stolen Bride

Whiskey Bay Brides

From Temptation to Twins
Twelve Nights of Temptation
His Temptation, Her Secret

Visit her Author Profile page at Harlequin.com, or barbaradunlop.com, for more titles.

For CJ Carmichael

One

As the bride and groom whirled into the first dance at the sumptuously decorated Beacon Hill Crystal Club, TJ Bauer struggled to block memories of his own wedding. It had been more than two years since Lauren had died, and there were days when he was at relative peace with her loss. But there were also days like this when the ache was so acute that his chest balled into a painful knot of loneliness.

"Doing okay?" Caleb Watford approached, handing TJ a glass of single malt, one ice cube, just the way TJ liked it.

"I'm fine."

"Liar."

TJ had no intention of getting into it, so he nodded to the dance floor instead. "Matt's one lucky man."

Caleb watched TJ's expression closely, as if he was

debating whether or not to let the topic drop. "I'll agree to that."

"It was touch and go there for a while." TJ forced his mind away from the memory of Lauren, reliving his good friend Matt Emerson's frantic, ring-less marriage proposal to Tasha, her packed suitcases at her feet. "I thought she was going to say no."

Caleb cracked a grin. "It all turned out in the end."

TJ found his own smile for Matt's good fortune. He was genuinely happy that his friend had found love. Tasha was smart, beautiful and completely down-to-earth. She was exactly what Matt needed in his life.

Caleb clapped a hand on TJ's shoulder. "You'll be next."

"Not." The cloud moved back over TJ's emotions.

"You need to keep an open mind."

"Would you replace Jules?"

The question brought silence.

TJ took a swallow of his drink. "That's what I thought."

"It's easy to say never when she's right here in front of me."

Both men shifted their gazes to Caleb's wife, Jules. She was radiant following the birth of her twin girls three months ago. Right now, she laughed at something her brother-in-law Noah said.

"It's hard to get past the never part," TJ said, struggling to put his feelings into words. He liked facts, not emotions. Emotions always tripped him up. "It's not that I'm not trying. I am. But it always cycles back to Lauren."

"I get it," Caleb said. "At least I think I get it. I know I can't possibly understand."

"If I could flip a switch…" TJ let the sentence drop.

Intellectually, he knew Lauren wasn't coming back. He even knew she'd want him to move on. But she was his true love, his one and only. He couldn't imagine anyone taking her place.

"Give it some more time," Caleb said.

"It's not like I have a choice," TJ responded, hearing the irony in his own tone. Time would march along no matter what he did or didn't do.

The strains of the song wound down to an end, and Matt and Tasha moved toward them, all smiles. Her graceful tulle skirt floated over the polished floor. TJ never thought he'd see the tomboyish marine mechanic in full bridal attire. When she wore a dress instead of coveralls, she was quite stunningly beautiful.

"Come and dance with the bride," she said to him, a tinkling laugh in her tone as she linked her arm with his.

"It would be an honor." As the best man, he put a smile on his face and set down his drink, determined to keep his melancholy thoughts to himself.

"Is everything okay?" she asked as they swung onto the dance floor.

Other couples joined them, and the dance floor filled as the music swelled.

"Everything is great," he said.

"I saw your expression when you were talking to Caleb."

"Where did you learn to dance like this?" TJ appreciated her concern, but this was *her* day. She didn't need to be worrying about him.

"What's going on, TJ?"

"Nothing. Well, one thing. I'm a little jealous of Matt."

"Now, that's a big fat lie."

He drew back slightly. "Look at yourself, Tasha. Every guy here is jealous of Matt."

She shook her head and laughed.

"Except for Caleb," TJ felt honor-bound to add. "And the other married guys… Well, some of them, anyway."

Now she looked amused. "That was a very carefully constructed compliment."

"It really went off the rails there, didn't it?"

"You just kept getting deeper and deeper."

"What I mean," he said, "is that you make a radiant bride."

"It's a very time-limited thing," she said.

It was his turn to laugh.

She put on a frown. "I can barely breathe in the corset, never mind walk in these heels. If there's an emergency, somebody's going to have to carry me out of here."

"I'm sure Matt will be happy to carry you anywhere you need to go."

She cast a glance at her new husband, and her expression turned to adoration. TJ felt a surge of envy at their obvious devotion to each other.

"Your mother seems delighted by the posh event," he said, switching his focus.

"I'm doing my duty as a daughter. But I've warned Matt, this may be the last time he sees me in a dress."

"You're going out on a high note."

TJ's phone vibrated in his tux pocket. He had it on silent, but Tasha obviously heard the low buzz.

"You can get that," she said.

"There's nobody I need to talk to right now."

"What if it's one of your investors?"

"It's Saturday night."

"It's Sunday morning in Australia." Tasha was aware of TJ's investment company's global reach.

"So, it's not a workday there either." He had no intention of interrupting the wedding reception with business.

The buzzing stopped.

"See?" he told her. "It went away."

"It always goes away when you don't pick up."

The phone buzzed again.

She stopped dancing. "You need to get that, TJ."

"No, I don't." He gently urged her to move.

"At least see who it is."

"It's nobody more important than you and Matt."

"It could be an emergency."

"Fine." He wasn't about to stand in the middle of the dance floor and argue with the bride.

He discreetly withdrew his phone and started dancing again.

Apparently appeased, she matched his movements.

Glancing down, he was surprised to see the call was from Seattle's St. Bea's Hospital. His company was a long-time contributor to Highside Hospital near his home in Whiskey Bay. But there was no affiliation with St. Bea's. He supposed someone could be soliciting a donation.

"Who is it?" Tasha asked.

He realized he'd stopped dancing again.

"St. Bea's Hospital."

A look of concern came over her face. "Someone could be hurt."

"I don't know why they'd take them to St. Bea's."

He was acquainted with a few people in Seattle, but most of his friends were in Whiskey Bay or Washington's capital city, Olympia, which was the closest major city. Even in Olympia, there was nobody who'd have him listed as an emergency contact.

The ringing stopped again.

"You better call them back," Tasha said. She linked her arm with his, steering him off the dance floor.

"Tasha," he protested.

"Humor me, or I'll worry."

"If that's what it takes." He hated being the cause of a disruption.

"That's what it takes."

At the edge of the floor, she moved away, giving him privacy.

TJ kept walking to the foyer, where the sound of the band was blocked, so it was quieter. He hit the callback button.

"St. Bea's Hospital, Oncology," a crisp female voice answered.

Oncology? Someone had cancer? "This is Travis Bauer. I'm returning a call from this number."

"Yes, Mr. Bauer. Let me put you through to Dr. Stannis."

"What is this—" TJ stopped talking when the line clicked and went silent.

He waited a few moments, not sure whether to be anxious or simply curious.

"Mr. Bauer?"

"Yes?"

"This is Dr. Shelley Stannis. I'm with the oncology transplant department here at St. Bea's."

A light came on for TJ. "Is this about a bone marrow donation?"

"Yes, it is. Thank you for calling back so quickly. Obviously, I got your information from the registry. We have a young leukemia patient here who is a potential match with you. If you're available, I'd like to set up a consultation and possibly final testing."

"How old?" It was the first question that came to TJ's mind.

"He's nine years old," she said.

TJ didn't hesitate. "When do you need me?"

"Are you saying you're willing to donate?"

"Absolutely."

"Do you have any questions?"

"I'm sure I will, although not right now. I'm in Boston. But I can come back."

There was a pause on the line. "If it's possible, Mr. Bauer, we'd like to do the tests tomorrow. As you can imagine, we have a very anxious mother hoping you'll turn out to be a close enough match."

"I'll be there. And please, call me TJ."

"Thank you very much, TJ."

"Of course. I'll see you tomorrow." He ended the call.

"Everything okay?" Matt had appeared beside him.

"Fine. Hopefully very fine. I may be a bone marrow match for a nine-year-old boy in Seattle."

It seemed to take Matt a moment to process the statement.

"I really hate to cut out on you," TJ said.

"Go!" Matt said, making a shooing motion with his hands. "Go, save a life."

TJ could feel his adrenaline come up with purpose. His next call was to a jet charter company he'd used in the past.

He didn't want to fight for a seat on a red-eye when a young boy and his mother were waiting. And he could afford to fly privately. There were moments in life when it came in handy to be a ridiculously wealthy man.

As she followed the wide corridor at St. Bea's Hospital, Sage Costas's heels echoed against the polished linoleum. Her stomach churned as it had for the past nine days while her son, Eli, had undergone a battery of tests and been diagnosed with an aggressive form of leukemia. The closer she came to the family lounge, the harder her heart pounded. She found herself wondering how much stress the human body could endure before it simply shut down.

She'd barely slept all week, hadn't slept at all last night. She'd forced herself to shower this morning and put on a little makeup. She didn't know why she thought makeup might help. But she wanted to make a good impression. She was terrified the donor would back out.

She could see him now. Through the lounge windows, she could see a tall, dark-haired, smartly dressed man talking to Dr. Stannis. He had to be the donor.

Her steps slowed, and she swallowed. Then she stopped at the closed door. It was more than she could do to push the handle. She'd prayed desperately for this moment. So much was at stake. She wasn't sure she could face it if the process fell apart.

She forced herself to open the door and step inside the lounge.

Dr. Stannis immediately spotted her. "Hello, Sage."

The man turned. His expression was instant bewilderment. "Sage?"

Her world tipped on its axis.

"Is that you?" he asked, stepping forward.

A roar came up in her ears. Her vision switched to black and white, then tunneled down to a pinhole.

"Sage?" Dr. Stannis moved quickly, taking her by the arm.

Sage's brain pulsed a million miles an hour. The room swayed for a moment, until her vision cleared.

He was still standing there.

"I'm fine," she managed to say around the lingering noise inside her head.

"Have you met TJ Bauer?" Dr. Stannis asked with obvious curiosity.

"We went to the same high school." Her voice was little more than a squeak.

How could this be happening?

"It's your son who's sick?" TJ's expression was filled with concern. "I'm so sorry, Sage."

Then his forehead creased, and she could all but see the calculations going on inside his head.

He turned to the doctor. "You said he was nine?"

"Yes."

TJ twisted slowly back to Sage, his words carefully enunciated. "And I'm a likely bone marrow match for him?"

Sage tried to swallow again, but her throat had gone paper dry.

TJ's eyes shifted from blue to gray thunder. "Is he my son?"

The doctor went still. The entire world went still. The ventilation system clicked against the booming silence.

All Sage could manage was a nod.

Dr. Stannis's grip firmed up on Sage's arm. "Perhaps we should sit down."

"I have a son?" TJ asked, his voice hoarse. "You got *pregnant*?"

Sage tried to speak. She managed to move her lips, but no sounds came out.

TJ wasn't having the same problem. "And you didn't *tell* me?"

Dr. Stannis jumped in. "I think it would be best if we all—"

Bitterness suddenly broke through Sage's fear. She found her voice, all but shouting. "You didn't deserve to know."

"Sage." Dr. Stannis's tone was shocked and sharp.

Sage immediately realized her mistake.

They were dependent on TJ. Eli's life depended on this man's good graces, this man who had deceived her, lied to her and taken shameless advantage of her teenage naïveté as a prank to amuse his friends.

She hated him. But he was the one person who could save her son's life.

"I'm sorry," she said, trying desperately to put some sincerity into her tone.

Judging by his expression, she hadn't pulled it off.

"Please don't…" Her stomach cramped up. "Please don't take it out on Eli."

He looked completely dumbfounded. Then he swore under his breath. "You actually think I'd harm a little boy…my own son—" He seemed to gather himself. "You think I'd let my anger with you impact my decision to donate? What kind of a man do you think I am?"

She didn't know what kind of a man he was. She knew what kind of a teenager he'd been back then— unscrupulous and self-centered. She had no reason to assume he'd changed.

"I don't know." She forced the words out.

"Well, *know*," he said. He looked to Dr. Stannis again. "How soon will we be sure I'm a close enough match?"

"A few days," she said. "But given the genetic connection, I'm even more optimistic."

"It's a stroke of luck," TJ said flatly.

Sage couldn't begin to guess at the emotion behind those words.

Dr. Stannis moved to look her directly in the eyes. "Are you sure you're all right?"

"I'm fine." For the moment, she was fine.

TJ was going to help them. They'd figure out the rest later. For now, the bone marrow transplant was all that mattered.

The doctor stepped back. "I'll give the two of you some time to talk."

With a final assessment of Sage's expression, she left the lounge.

Sage had no idea what to say next, and the seconds ticked past.

When TJ finally spoke, there was contained fury in his tone. "I'm not going to ask you how you could have done something so horrible."

"Me?" Sage could barely believe he'd said it. "You were there. You know *exactly* what happened between us."

He waved a dismissive hand. "That was a stupid stunt by an ignorant kid. We've grown up since then. You've known about this for a *decade*."

"You were a shallow, self-centered jerk."

He squared his shoulders and set his square jaw. "I don't want to fight with you, Sage. This conversation can wait. Right now, I want to meet my son."

Sage staggered and reached to an armchair for support. "No."

"What do you mean no? No is no longer an option for you."

She struggled for the right words. "You can't tell him, TJ. Not now. Not while he's so sick." She stretched her arm expansively toward the door to the rest of the hospital. "There's no way we can expect him to absorb news like that in the middle of all this."

TJ seemed to consider her words. His expression lost its hard edge. "I need to meet him, Sage. We don't have to tell him I'm his father, at least not right away. But I'm going to meet him, and I'm not waiting another minute."

Sage decided she could live with that. "Okay."

"His name is Eli?"

"Yes. Eli Thomas Costas."

TJ didn't react to the name. He walked over to the lounge door and pulled it open, holding it for her. "Take me to my son."

"Whoa, whoa, back up, back up," Matt said to TJ. "You say he's *nine* years old?"

"It was in high school," TJ responded.

There was an open beer on the wide arm of his wooden deck chair on Matt's Whiskey Bay Marina sundeck, but TJ had no interest in drinking it.

"So, before you met Lauren," Caleb said.

The three men were sitting around the gas fire pit, but it was early on a June evening, so they hadn't bothered lighting it.

"I didn't cheat on Lauren." TJ's tone was hard.

"I'm just getting the time line straight."

"It was a one-night thing. At prom. We danced."

TJ didn't want to own up to participating in the foolish prank that had led him to ask nerdy brainiac Sage Costas to dance with him that night. At least not until he had to. And he hoped that was never.

"And she never told you about the baby?" Matt asked.

"I assume that's rhetorical," TJ replied.

If Sage had told him about Eli, TJ would have moved heaven and earth to have a relationship with his son. TJ's own father had walked out before TJ was born, and there was no way he'd do that to a child of his own.

"What's he like?" Caleb asked, his tone dropping.

TJ's mind went back to the sleepy boy in the stark hospital bed. "He's a great-looking kid."

Eli had been too tired to do much but say hello.

"Like his dad?" Matt joked.

TJ would be lying if he said he hadn't seen some of himself in Eli. He didn't think he was imagining it.

"If he's got his mother's brains, the world better watch out." As he said the words, TJ realized they were entirely true. From a genetic perspective, Eli had a fantastic mother. Back in high school, Sage was voted most likely to save the world or become president.

"When are you going to tell him?" Matt asked.

TJ decided it was time for a shot of alcohol, no matter how weak. He raised his beer and took a drink before answering. "I don't know. When he's feeling better, I guess."

"And the tests?"

"They said the results will take a couple of days. I've got three major private placement deals on the table. I have to close them. Then I'm clearing my desk to go back to Seattle. Whatever happens, if I'm a match or not, he's still my kid, and he's getting the best medical care money can buy."

Matt and Caleb exchanged a look.

"What?" TJ asked.

"That's a good place for your money," Matt said.

"You bet it's a good place for my money."

But money wasn't the only thing his son needed. TJ didn't know what he'd do if he wasn't a bone marrow match. He had to be a match. Nothing else was acceptable.

"You talked to him?" Caleb asked.

"Only a little. He was pretty groggy from all the medication. Sage says he plays baseball, a catcher."

"Have you talked to a lawyer?" Matt asked.

"I've talked to three lawyers." TJ's company Tide Rush Investments had a financial lawyer on retainer and his firm had a family law division.

"What do they say?"

"That I've got a case."

"What are you looking to get?" Matt asked.

"What has she offered?" Caleb's brow shot up.

TJ took another pull on his beer. It was such an incredibly ordinary thing to do—sitting up here with his two friends like he had hundreds of times over the years. But his life had been turned upside down. It would never be the same again.

He'd been considering his position for the past thirty-six hours. "She had custody for the first nine years. I'll take the next nine."

Caleb frowned.

"You can't take that hard a line," Matt said.

"A teenage boy needs his dad. I'd have given anything to have my old man show up in my life when I was Eli's age," TJ said. He had a lot of time to make up for, and he had no intention of letting Sage or anyone else stop him.

"They need their mom too," Caleb said.

TJ knew that. But he didn't want to admit it right now. He wanted to hold on to his anger at Sage for a while.

"She can have visitation," he said. "That's more than she gave me."

"Could you move to Seattle?" Matt asked.

"The Whiskey Bay school is top-notch," TJ countered. "So is the area hospital. And the lifestyle can't be beat." He couldn't imagine a more perfect place to raise a child.

"The neighbors are pretty good," Caleb said with a half smile.

"It's not like I don't have the room."

His wife, Lauren, had wanted several children. She'd designed a six-bedroom house with a massive recreation area in the basement for rainy days and a nanny suite over the garage. She'd been trying to get pregnant when she was diagnosed with breast cancer.

"I can't see it being that straightforward." There was a cautionary note to Matt's voice.

"Nothing's that straightforward," TJ said. "But I'm a determined and resourceful man."

"She's the mother of your child."

"And I'm the father of hers—a fact she seems to have conveniently ignored."

"Do you know why?" Caleb asked. "Why she kept it from you? I mean, she could easily have come after you for child support."

"She wouldn't have had to *come after* me. I'd have stepped up without a fight."

"I know. I know. But you'd think she'd have wanted your help."

TJ knew the whole truth would eventually come out. His friends were too astute, and they cared too much about him to let him get away with a vague explanation. It was both a blessing and a curse.

TJ took the plunge. "She said I didn't deserve to know about Eli."

"Why?" Caleb's question was perfectly predictable.

"Because it was a prank."

Both of his friends looked at him blankly.

"Prom night." TJ gritted his teeth at the memory. "A group of us, the seniors on the football team, we each picked a girl's name out of a hat. I picked Sage."

"I'm guessing they weren't the girls on the cheerleading squad," Matt said. His disappointment in TJ was obvious.

TJ knew he deserved that. "Not the cheerleading squad. They were the nerds, the brains. It was supposed to be a kiss, only a dance and a kiss. That was it. But Sage…"

He remembered the overpowering rush of adolescent hormones. He couldn't say what it was about her. She had been thin and freckled, with this wild red hair. But when he'd kissed her, she'd kissed him back, and they'd both been left breathless. His car had been far too close to the side door of the gym, and they'd ended up in the back seat.

"We can fill in the rest," Caleb said.

"I tracked her down the next day to apologize. But she'd already heard about the prank. She was enraged, punched me square in the chest." TJ's hand went reflexively to the spot where her small fist had connected. "She told me she never wanted to speak to me again."

"You can't blame her," Matt said.

"It was stupid and cruel, I know. But I only planned to kiss her. The rest of it was on both of us. It was more than just consensual. And she's kept my son from me for nine years. The two things don't even compare."

Two

A week later, mere hours after the transplant procedure, Sage expected to find TJ lounging in his hospital bed. But he was up and halfway dressed, reaching his arms into a crisp white dress shirt.

"Should you be out of bed?" she asked, stepping past the curtain.

"The nurse took the IV out a few minutes ago."

"But you just had surgery."

"I'm aware of that." He adjusted his collar and shifted the lapels across what she'd noted was a magnificently muscular chest.

"You must be sore." She couldn't believe he'd bounce back this fast.

"Only my hip. Dr. Stannis says it'll disappear in a few days. Hanging around here isn't going to help any."

"Can you drive?" Sage asked.

She didn't know where he was staying, but she wanted to be sure he got safely back to his hotel. It was the least she could do—the very least she could do for the man who may have saved her son's life.

"They didn't serve liquor in the operating room."

"You know what I mean. You must be woozy."

"It's not too bad." He finished doing up his buttons. "I'm not crazy about anesthetic. I like my brain cells too much."

"I'm sorry you had to go through that." She struggled to keep her emotions at bay. "Thank you, TJ."

He sent her a sharp gaze, trapping hers for a long second. "You don't have to thank me. He's my son. You don't ever have to thank me for helping my son."

It would be a struggle for her to get used to that. She'd had Eli to herself for such a long time, she couldn't imagine letting anyone else into their circle.

"I need you to understand that, Sage."

"You're going to have to give me some time."

"I've already wasted nine years." TJ took a pewter-gray blazer from a hanger on the wall and put it on over his designer outfit.

She was terrified to ask him what he had in mind. She didn't want to have that conversation. "They're watching Eli for signs of rejection," she said instead.

"Anything yet?" TJ asked.

"It's too soon to tell. Are you staying in Seattle overnight?"

Again, he pasted her with the sharp look. "I'm staying here as long as it takes."

"Takes to what?"

He turned his back to her, punching a code into a small safe on the wall and retrieving his wallet and keys.

Then he faced her and deposited the wallet into his inside jacket pocket. He kept the keys in his hand.

"I've been thinking," he said.

She worriedly searched his expression for a clue. "About…"

"I'd like to move Eli to Highside Hospital."

The words blindsided her. "What? Where?"

"It's near Whiskey Bay. It's state-of-the-art—"

"No."

"Hear me out."

Protective instincts rose inside her, along with a healthy dose of fear. "You're not taking Eli out of Seattle."

"It's the best place for him. I've donated to Highside for years, and they have the best doctors, the best technology, he'd be—"

"St. Bea's is a fantastic hospital."

"It's a public hospital."

Her tone went up in defense. "So what?"

"So, they're busy, overworked, stretched for resources."

"They've given Eli everything he needs. They diagnosed him. They found *you*." She stopped, realizing TJ's unique role in Eli's recovery might not be her strongest argument.

"I was in the registry. Any hospital would have found me."

"I don't want him moved." She needed to be close to her son while he recovered.

Whiskey Bay was three hours away. She'd missed so much time at work these past weeks, she couldn't take much more off. She'd planned to work as many hours as she could while Eli was recovering.

"It'll free up a bed for someone who desperately needs it," TJ said.

"What part of no don't you understand?"

"What part of *father* don't *you* understand?"

"He can't be moved yet." She realized her best argument was the medical one.

"I'm not talking about today, or even tomorrow. But as soon as he's strong enough, we can hire a medical helicopter. It'll take thirty minutes, tops."

"Just like that?" She resisted an urge to snap her fingers.

"Just like what?"

"You'll hire a helicopter."

"It's fast. It'll be comfortable. The onboard medics are equipped for anything."

"It'll cost a *fortune*."

His expression was a study in incomprehension. "It's my son's health we're talking about."

She was back in high school again. "You're still the big man, aren't you?"

His nostrils flared, but he didn't answer.

"The star athlete, the guy who got anything he wanted, grants, scholarships, the best parties, all the girls."

TJ opened his mouth, but she didn't let him interrupt.

"The wide receiver with the magic hands, who was going all-state, who could write his own ticket."

"I'm not going to apologize for getting a college degree."

Sage felt like a knife had been shoved into her heart. She'd given up countless scholarship offers to raise Eli.

"I earned my money," TJ continued. "I'm spending it on my son."

She stepped forward. "Your son doesn't need it."

"You want to fight me on this?"

Sage was about to say yes, when the curtain was whisked open.

Dr. Stannis appeared. She looked TJ up and down and smiled. "Nice bounce-back."

"I've been through worse," he said. "How's Eli?"

"He's still in recovery. We're going to keep him there for a few more hours. Do you feel ready for discharge?"

"Absolutely. When can we see him?"

"Later tonight." Dr. Stannis glanced at her watch. "Nine-ish? But he'll still be pretty groggy until morning."

"We'll come back at nine."

Sage was about to protest that she wasn't leaving.

"Make sure you get plenty of fluids," Dr. Stannis said to TJ.

"Is there a good restaurant nearby?"

It took Sage a second to realize the question was for her. "I'm, uh, not sure."

He looked puzzled.

She wasn't about to explain to Mr. Moneybags Helicopter Charter that she normally brought snacks from home to save money over eating in the hospital cafeteria. Forget restaurants. They weren't even on her radar.

"The Red Grill is just down the road," Dr. Stannis said. "It gets good reviews from families of our patients."

"Done," TJ said. He motioned for Sage to go first.

She didn't understand.

"I'm buying," he told her. "We have to eat."

"Fluids," Dr. Stannis said. "For both of you." She gave Sage a pointed look.

They'd had a few conversations about the fact that Sage had lost some weight these past weeks.

"Does Cabernet Sauvignon count?" TJ asked with a teasing smile.

"Only in moderation." Dr. Stannis waved her pen. "Water's better. Tea would be perfect."

"Yes, ma'am."

"And make sure Sage eats."

TJ looked down at Sage with a curious expression. "Anything in particular?"

"Calories."

"Lasagna it is," he said.

"I don't like lasagna." Sage did like lasagna, but she was still thrown off balance by TJ's determination to move Eli to a different hospital. And she resented the way he was organizing her dinner.

"Then order something else," he said easily. "They'll have a menu."

"I'm aware of how restaurants work."

"Good. Then you won't mind taking advantage of one. You are a little thin."

"I'm not thin." She was conveniently ignoring the fact that her favorite jeans were sagging at her waist.

"I didn't mean it as an insult."

"Your opinion means nothing to me."

Dr. Stannis broke in. "And I will see you two later."

"Thank you, Doctor." TJ gave her hand a warm shake with both of his.

Sage wished she could hug the doctor, but she settled for shaking as well. "Thank you *so* much."

"You're most welcome." Dr. Stannis's sincerity was unquestionable. "Go take care of yourself for a couple of hours. Eli is in excellent hands."

"I know," Sage said.

She had complete confidence in the staff at St. Bea's. There wasn't a reason in the world for TJ to move Eli anywhere else.

* * *

The Red Grill turned out to have a Southwest flair, with bright colors and lively music in the dining room. The hostess seated them on the patio, which was quieter. She quickly brought them glasses of iced tea and tortilla chips with guacamole.

The pain in TJ's hip was getting worse, but he didn't want to muddle his thinking with any more painkillers. He pushed the tortilla chips toward Sage, but she shook her head.

"Doctor's orders," he said.

She gave him a glare but took a chip and bit down on it.

TJ had so many things to ask her, he barely knew where to start. "Do you have any pictures of Eli?"

She set the chip on her side plate. "I do." She dug into her small bag and retrieved her phone, opening the photo app.

When she handed it over, TJ got the first look at his infant son. The pain in his hip faded as he took in the smiling, cherubic baby.

"How old is he here?" TJ asked.

"Six months in that first one."

He stared at the picture for a long time.

"Are you ready to order?" the waitress interrupted.

"We'll need a few minutes," Sage answered for them.

TJ flipped to the next picture. Toddler Eli was standing in a yard, petting a black Lab that was taller than him.

"You have a dog?" TJ asked.

"No. They're not allowed in our basement suite. Beaumont belonged to a friend. Eli loves animals. He talked me into a gerbil once."

"What happened?"

"He played with it every day, but it was kind of sad. It just wasn't the same as having a dog to walk and play fetch with. Eventually, the gerbil died and, well, we weren't really supposed to have it in the first place. And I didn't want to get evicted, so we never got another."

"A boy deserves a dog." TJ could remember how badly he'd wanted a dog when he was a boy.

"A boy deserves a roof over his head," Sage retorted.

TJ looked up from the screen to see her annoyed expression. "I didn't mean that as a criticism."

"I tried, TJ."

"I know you did. I'm sure you did. I don't understand why you didn't contact me."

"Well, I'm not going to explain it all over again."

The waitress arrived once more.

"I'll take a beef burrito," TJ said, not wanting to bother reading the menu and not caring what he ate.

"The same," Sage said, and the waitress departed.

"You didn't look at the menu," he noted.

"Just so long as it's not lasagna."

He couldn't tell if she was joking or not. He flipped to the next picture.

Eli was in front of a birthday cake covered in blue icing and decorated with mini balloons. There were three candles on the cake, and he was grinning ear to ear.

"His birthday?" TJ asked, although it was pretty obvious.

Sage nodded.

Eli had dark, slightly wavy hair, just like TJ's. There was a familiarity in his eyes and in his slightly crooked smile. TJ's chest was tight. His heart was expanding to fill every crack and crevice behind his rib cage.

He had a son—his own son. He'd missed so much of Eli's life.

He moved to the next picture, but it blurred in front of his eyes. "I deserve a chance to catch up."

She looked like she wanted to argue. But then she looked like she didn't have it in her.

"I know," she said. "You can see him as much as you want. I won't try to stop you."

"I want him at Highside Hospital."

This time, she shook her head, and he could see the steel determination in her eyes. "That's not possible. He needs me. He needs me there every day."

"You can stay in Whiskey Bay." The problem was hardly insurmountable.

"I have a job, TJ. I can appreciate this is a huge adjustment for you, but—"

"Adjustment? You call what I'm going through an *adjustment*?" He shifted in his chair, and pain shot through his hip. He struggled to keep his expression neutral.

"You're in pain," she said. "Should we go back to the hospital?"

"No!" He lowered his voice. "We should eat. Starving yourself isn't going to help Eli."

Her jaw clenched tight. "Are you going to give me parenting advice?"

"I'm not." He leaned forward to make his point. "Because I have no idea what it's *like* to be a parent, thanks to you."

"I just apologized."

"You think that cuts it?" He realized his tone was growing louder, and he forced himself to take a beat. They were both raw and tired, and sniping at each other wasn't going to help anything.

Their burritos arrived, along with condiments and utensils.

He slid her phone back across the table. "Thank you for showing me the pictures."

She looked like she wanted to say something more, but she stayed silent.

"You should eat," he told her.

She gave a jerky nod.

He flagged down the waitress. "Can I get a shot of tequila?"

"Painkillers would work better," Sage said.

"It's not for the pain."

They ate in silence for a while.

Despite everything, TJ couldn't help but think it was good she was eating something. He might not agree with her decision to keep him in the dark, but she'd obviously been through a lot taking care of a sick child all on her own.

Then it occurred to him that she might not be on her own. She didn't wear a wedding ring, and her last name remained the same, but that didn't mean she wasn't in a relationship, or even married for that matter.

"Are you single?" he asked bluntly.

Her eyes widened in obvious surprise.

"Is there a man, somebody in your and Eli's lives?" he elaborated. It would certainly give her a good reason for keeping TJ out of the picture.

"No. There's nobody. It's just me and Eli." There was an echo of loneliness in the statement.

"Your family?"

He didn't know if she had siblings. He didn't recall any from high school. But it was a pretty big place, and he certainly hadn't known the entire student body.

"My parents died a few years ago. Not that they were in the picture anyway."

"Did they live out of state?"

"No. They cut me out of their lives. They didn't want me to keep Eli."

TJ's horror was instant.

"They wanted me to give him up for adoption."

"Why?"

"They weren't willing to help me with him and they didn't think I could do it on my own. But they were wrong." Her gaze was firm on him. "I walked out of the house at six months pregnant and never saw them again."

She should have contacted him. Why on earth hadn't she contacted him?

"It was the right choice," she continued. "For all our struggles, I'd do it again in a heartbeat."

He couldn't seem to stop himself. "I wish you'd done some things different."

Her knuckles appeared white as she gripped her knife and fork. "I can't go back in time, TJ."

"I know." He'd lost his appetite, but he forced himself to keep eating.

They could only go forward. And for that, he needed to be at his strongest. If there was anything on earth he could do to help Eli, he was going to do it.

Sage fought the urge to take TJ's hand. It was an irrational urge, since their relationship for the past twenty-four hours could best be described as an armed truce. But her nerves were strung tight as they waited for Dr. Stannis to bring them Eli's test results.

The guest chairs in Dr. Stannis's office were jade-green leather. They were cushioned and comfortable.

The room was decorated in muted earth tones, a painting here, some pottery there. It didn't look sterile, not like a waiting room. She couldn't help but imagine it was designed to keep people calm, people like her who were waiting for life-and-death results, or who were hearing the worst kind of news.

"Hey." TJ's tone was soft, and he was the one who took her hand.

She turned to look at him.

"Don't do that to yourself," he said.

He gave her hand a squeeze, which inexplicably made her feel better.

"It's going to be all good," he said.

"You don't know that." Her voice was dry, high-pitched. She tried to swallow, but she couldn't.

He came out of the chair, on one knee in front of her, taking both her hands in his. "Positive thoughts," he said, his voice as gentle as she'd ever heard.

She managed a nod, but she was terrified to be optimistic, as if karma would reach out and smack her if she dared to hope.

The door opened, and Dr. Stannis entered the room. "I won't keep you in suspense," she said briskly, breezing toward her desk. "The results are what we were hoping for. There are no signs of rejection or infection at this point."

Sage thought she might faint with relief.

Before she could move, TJ's arms were around her. He drew her to her feet and hugged her tight.

"Yes," his deep voice hissed next to her ear. "Yes."

His body was strong and solid against hers, warm and welcoming. She was suddenly transported back ten years, to their dance, their kiss, the acute and unexplainable feeling she'd had of coming home, like she belonged in TJ's arms, like she'd been waiting her whole life to be held by him.

She hadn't been able to let go then, and she didn't want to let go now. It was a frightening feeling, and she tried to pull back.

TJ didn't seem to want to let her go either. He held on tight for long seconds before breaking his grip.

"He did it," he said.

"You did it," Sage said.

At the moment, she didn't care who TJ was, what he'd done in the past or what he might do in the future. He'd saved her son, and she owed him everything.

"He needs to get his strength back," Dr. Stannis said.

Sage felt a dampness on her cheek and swiped at it with the back of her hand. She hadn't even realized she was crying.

"And we'll have to carefully monitor his T cells. Infection is still a very serious concern." Dr. Stannis dropped into her high-backed chair. "But at this point, all signs are positive."

TJ eased Sage back into her chair and then took his own.

"How long until he can come home?" she asked. She couldn't wait to have Eli back in his own bed.

"Normally, we'd wait a week," Dr. Stannis said. "But in Eli's case, I'm recommending two."

Sage's euphoria disappeared. "Something is wrong?"

"The chemo was very hard on him. And we've already fought one infection. He's young, and his body has been through a lot."

"Are you sure that's all?"

"I would tell you if there was anything else."

"What about another hospital?" TJ asked.

Sage wanted to shout *no*.

Dr. Stannis switched her attention to TJ. "What do you mean?"

"Highside Hospital, on the coast."

"They're top-notch. There's no doubt about that," Dr. Stannis said.

"I'm affiliated with them," TJ said. "They're world renowned. I want to do everything possible to support his recovery."

Dr. Stannis looked at Sage. "Medically speaking, yes, he could be moved there."

"He'd have a private room," TJ said to Sage. "It would be quieter for him while he recovered. Their equipment is state-of-the-art. If Eli came down with an infection or any other complication, he'd be in the best possible facility."

Sage's hands began to shake. "He wouldn't have his mother."

"You'd come with him. They have a residential facility for parents. You can stay there the whole time free of charge."

"I have a job," Sage protested. There was no way she could take another two weeks off. "After he's out, once he's better, the two of you can—"

"This isn't about me seeing him." TJ's tone was firm. "This is about Eli getting the best care. The nurse-to-patient ratio in Highside is the lowest in the country. They have a pediatric ICU, an extensive on-site laboratory system, and they're an oncology teaching facility."

Dr. Stannis rose to her feet. "I'll leave the two of you to talk."

"One more question," TJ said to Dr. Stannis.

"Of course."

"If Eli was your son, would you choose St. Bea's or Highside?"

Dr. Stannis's hesitation and her guilty look in Sage's direction answered the question.

"I have to be honest," Dr. Stannis said. "Highside is unrivaled for patient care and outcomes."

"Thank you," TJ said.

Dr. Stannis left the office.

"I have to work while he's recovering," Sage said to TJ. "I can't do that from Whiskey Bay." Surely a mother's love counted for something.

"Take some time off. Don't worry about money, I can—"

"It's not just the money." She was embarrassed that her voice cracked. "I've missed so much time lately. They're trying to be patient with me, but they're going to have to replace me if I don't get back there soon."

"Where do you work?"

She found herself raising her chin. "The Eastway Community Center. I'm their event planner."

She wasn't embarrassed by her job. She did meaningful work that helped people in need. But she knew it was nothing compared to what TJ had accomplished since high school.

"Maybe I can talk to them."

"Oh, no, you don't." The idea was offensive. She was an adult. She didn't need some tall, male financial mogul in an expensive suit to advocate on her behalf. "Eli's home is here. His mother is here. My *life* is here."

"And *my* life is—" TJ suddenly stopped talking. He rocked back in his chair, looking annoyed with himself. "Fine. I'll let it drop."

"Thank you." She was grateful he'd seen the light.

"Right now, we should check on Eli."

She was all for that. "Yes." She nodded rapidly. "Yes."

TJ came to his feet. "We can talk about it some more later."

"Wait. What?" She didn't want to revisit an argument she'd just won.

"I haven't changed my mind. But I'm not unreasonable."

"Not changing your mind *is* being unreasonable." She stood.

"Not if I change yours."

"You won't change mine." Of that, she was positive. If that was what he was waiting for, she was home free. She headed for the door.

It was a ten-minute walk from Dr. Stannis's office to the pediatrics wing. It was almost dinner, and Sage was hoping to coax Eli to eat something, maybe a little Jell-O. He liked red the best.

She couldn't wait for the day when his appetite returned, then his strength and his energy. She couldn't wait for the day when he was an ordinary little boy all over again.

Three

Once again, TJ was struck by how small and pale Eli looked in the stark white hospital bed. But at least this time he was sitting up. He had a comic book in his lap, and he was slowly turning the pages.

He heard them come in, and he looked up.

"Hi, Mom," he said in a quiet voice.

"Hello, sweetheart." Sage approached his bed and gave him a kiss on the forehead.

There were three other beds in the room. Two were occupied. One with a young girl whose leg was in traction due to a car accident, another by a boy who TJ had learned had his appendix taken out and was in the process of being discharged.

The hospital was spick-and-span. But it was also showing its age, with noisy heaters, worn linoleum and lights that flickered and buzzed overhead. The privacy curtains were a faded yellow, and the table trays squeaked when they were wheeled to a new position.

"Hi, Eli," TJ said.

Eli looked past Sage to meet TJ's eyes. He was clearly puzzled by TJ's continued presence at his bedside. TJ didn't blame the kid. It likely didn't make much sense to Eli for a stranger to show up and keep hanging around while he recovered.

Sage had introduced TJ as an old friend from high school. TJ was dying to tell Eli the truth. But he respected Sage's request to wait until Eli was stronger.

"Hi," Eli answered shortly, looking annoyed.

"How are you feeling?" Sage asked, straightening.

Eli shrugged.

"Are you hungry?" Sage asked.

"Not really." Eli looked back down at the comic book.

"You need to build up your strength." She smoothed his slightly ragged hair.

"I'll try," he said.

"Are you frustrated by the slow progress?" TJ asked.

Sage didn't take the single seat beside the bed, and he wasn't about to sit down and let her stand, so the black vinyl chair was just in the way. TJ maneuvered around it.

Eli shifted to watch his progress. "Are you dating my mom?"

"What?" Sage gasped. "What makes you ask that?"

"No," TJ answered. "I'm not dating your mom. We're old friends."

Sage sat down in the chair and put her hand on Eli's shoulder. "There's something you should know, honey."

TJ stopped breathing.

Eli looked at Sage. "What?"

"TJ donated the bone marrow for your transplant."

TJ let out his breath. He was disappointed, of course. But it had seemed like an abrupt way to tell Eli TJ was his father. It was better that they wait. This was enough.

Eli's eyes opened a little wider. "Are you serious?"

"Yes." Sage took his hand and gave it a kiss. "TJ was your donor."

Eli looked embarrassed. His gaze focused tentatively on TJ's.

"I was more than happy to help," TJ assured him.

Eli's slim shoulders squared, and he seemed to sit up a little straighter. "Thank you, sir."

TJ's heart swelled with pride. "I'm just glad you're getting better."

Eli's expression faltered. "Am I?"

"Of course you are," Sage said, concern clear in her tone.

"I don't feel better."

"You're sitting up."

Eli glanced around the bed, as if the significance of sitting up hadn't occurred to him.

"You couldn't sit up yesterday," Sage said.

"I couldn't, could I?"

"You *are* getting better," she told him firmly.

"It's only a matter of time," TJ said.

Eli gave a ghost of a smile. "I thought they were lying."

"Who?" Sage asked.

"Dr. Stannis. The nurses. They keep saying these things take time, and I should relax and let my body heal."

"They're right."

"That's what they said to Joey." Eli's eyes went glassy

with unshed tears. "They told him that right up to when he died."

TJ felt like he'd been sucker punched.

A stricken expression on her face, Sage rose and drew Eli into her arms. "Oh, sweetheart."

"It would be okay," Eli said. "I mean, I'd deal with it if it happened."

"The transplant was a success," Sage said with firm conviction.

"You don't have to deal with it," TJ said. Then he re-thought his words.

Eli had plenty to deal with for the next few months.

"It's going to be tough," TJ told his son. "You'll need to be strong. But you are most definitely getting better."

"I can read again," Eli said. "At least a little bit without my head feeling like a baseball hit it."

"I hear you play baseball," TJ said, perching on the corner of the bed.

"I used to," Eli said.

"That's something to look forward to."

"Over the long-term," Sage said.

TJ couldn't tell if it was a rebuke or if she was just carrying on with the conversation.

"For now," she continued, "maybe we can look forward to some Jell-O?"

Eli thought about it for a moment. "I can try."

"Good for you."

TJ found himself smiling at the simple accomplishment. "Is there anything you feel like?" he asked Eli. "Anything at all?"

Eli looked to his mom as if seeking permission. "Could I have a chocolate milkshake?"

"I can run out and pick one up," TJ offered.

"Yes." Sage surreptitiously swiped her hand across her cheeks. "Yes, darling. You can have as many chocolate milkshakes as you want."

"Finally," Eli said with a small smile. "Something good in the hospital."

TJ couldn't believe his son was making a joke. In a hospital bed, weak and frightened, and fighting for his life, he was making a joke. His kid had mettle. Again, pride rose in his chest.

He left the room and took the elevator to the main lobby. There was a fast-food restaurant down the block that served milkshakes. But Eli deserved better than any old milkshake. TJ wanted his first gift to his son to be at least a little bit special.

So he drove to a gourmet ice-cream shop ten minutes away and waited while they made a custom order.

When TJ got back, Eli was semi-reclined in his bed. His eyes were closed, and he was listening to Sage read a story. She was sitting between Eli's bed and the bed of the little girl with the broken leg.

The girl looked to have other injuries too, TJ realized. One of her arms was bandaged, and she had a brace on her other leg.

She looked shyly at the milkshake, and TJ felt like the biggest heel in the world.

Sage stopped reading.

TJ set the milkshake on Eli's table.

"Is there something you'd like?" he asked the girl, moving closer.

"Heidi, this is my friend TJ," Sage said to the girl.

"Hi, Heidi." He offered her a smile. "I should have asked you before. What would you like to eat? As long as it's okay with the nurses, I can bring you anything."

She hesitated.

"Go ahead," Sage told her. "He's rich. He can afford something great."

TJ was taken aback by Sage's description of him. It was true, but it was an odd thing to tell a child.

"Pizza?" she asked shyly.

"Absolutely," TJ answered. "What kind do you like?"

"Hawaiian," she said. "And…" She bit her bottom lip.

"What else?" he asked. "Do you want a soda?"

"Can I have extra cheese?"

"Extra cheese it is." Out of the corner of his eye, TJ saw Eli lift the milkshake to his lips.

Heidi's blue eyes lit up with simple joy.

"This is really good," Eli said.

"Fantastic," TJ said to Eli. He hadn't felt this good about a gift in years.

"I can get you a milkshake, too," he said to Heidi.

Instead of answering, she looked to Sage with amazement.

"Chocolate or vanilla?" Sage asked her. "Or maybe strawberry or caramel?"

"Caramel," Heidi said, sounding breathless.

"What about you?" TJ asked Sage, not about to mess this up a second time. "Pizza and milkshakes all around?"

Sage gave him a grin, and he swore he could feel her joy seep into his very pores.

"You bet," she said. "Surprise me."

"I'm on it." He gave them all a mock salute and walked out of the hospital room feeling ridiculously like a superhero.

After the pizza and milkshakes, Sage read aloud until both Eli and Heidi were sleeping. Then she said good-night to the nurse before she and TJ walked to the lobby. She was tired, but she was also relieved. Eli was showing definite signs of improvement. He'd finished his entire milkshake and even had a couple bites of pizza.

"I'll be back tomorrow morning," TJ said as they approached the bank of glass doors.

"I know you will."

They were going to have to work this out somehow. But for now, the best she could do was one day at a time.

"Where's your car?" he asked, stopping as she turned left on the sidewalk.

The parking lot was to the right.

"I'm taking the bus."

He closed the gap between them. "Why would you do that?"

She didn't want to tell him. But she didn't want to make a big deal about it either.

She kept her tone blasé, matter-of-fact. "I don't have a car."

He blinked. "Who doesn't have a car?"

"Me."

"Why?"

"Because I don't."

"How do you get to work?"

She could hear the diesel engine and the air brakes of a bus coming up the hill. She pointed to it.

"That's crazy," he said.

She didn't like it much, but she'd sold her car a month ago when they'd started doing tests on Eli. Their meager insurance policy didn't begin to cover all the costs.

"You need a car," he said with authority.

"I had a car."

"Did you crash it?"

"*No*, I didn't crash it. I sold it."

"Why would you—" He stopped, and his brows rose. "The medical bills."

"Yes, the medical bills."

There was no point in pretending. She was a single mother with a low-paying job and a sick child. Of all the things she had going for her in life, money wasn't one of them.

"As of this second," TJ said, "there are no medical bills. You have no medical bills."

"You can't—"

"I can, and I am. How much have you paid so far?"

"None of your business."

"You want me to guess?"

"No, I don't want you to guess." It was her pride arguing with him. There was no practical purpose for insisting on footing the bill herself. From everything she knew, he had money to burn.

"I'll drive you home."

"I have a bus pass."

"It's nearly eleven. You're not getting on the bus."

She folded her arms over her chest. "I'm a functioning adult, TJ. I don't need you or anyone else to take care of me. I've been on this bus dozens of times at night. And I don't need your permission to do it again."

"I'm offering you a simple favor."

"You're…" She paused. She was exhausted, and it was twenty minutes until the Number Seven bus arrived. She had to transfer at the downtown station, which would mean an additional fifteen-minute wait before she boarded the final bus. She was being a fool to turn him down.

She closed her eyes for a second. "Okay. Thank you. That will be quicker."

"Are you always this stubborn?"

She gave him a glare.

"I mean good. My car is this way." He pointed to the south lot.

"I'm used to being self-reliant," she said, although she didn't owe him an explanation.

"Your life has changed," he said.

"So has yours."

He used his remote to unlock the doors to a low-slung red sports car.

"Drastically," she added, contrasting it to the fifteen-year-old minivan she'd recently sold.

He opened the passenger door and stood waiting for her to get in. "We're in this together, Sage."

She didn't like his phrasing. "We have a common interest."

"We have a child together."

She didn't have another response, so she got into the car.

The seats were smooth leather, cool and comfortable, cradling her body, filling the car with a subtle earthy scent. The navigation screen and dashboard made her think of a space shuttle. The seat belt came out smoothly, clipping effortlessly together.

TJ swung into the driver's seat.

"Where to?" he asked, pressing the start button.

"North on Fairton Road."

"You live downtown?"

"It's close to work."

Her rented basement suite was in an older part of the city. Gentrification was taking place near the water, but it hadn't yet made it to Fir Street. That kept rent low, for which she was grateful. But the nearby development was also pushing trouble closer and closer to her block.

TJ paid the parking charges and exited the lot.

It was a short drive to the highway, and there their speed increased.

The ride was smooth, and the sports car hugged the road. It was like floating on a cushion of air. It was so much better than the bus. She leaned her head back against the soft headrest and watched the strobe of streetlights above.

Too soon, they came to her exit.

She directed him to her neighborhood and pointed out the right house.

He pulled to the curb, setting the brake and shutting off the engine. He stared through the windshield. "Who are those guys?"

As she unbuckled her seat belt, Sage took in a group of teens and young adults in front of the corner market. There were six of them, scruffy-looking, all male. A couple of them were smoking, another couple were showing an interest in TJ's car.

"They look worse than they are." Sage had never been bothered by anyone.

"Are there a lot of drugs around here?"

"How would I know?"

He gave her a frown.

"No more and no less than in other parts of the city. I don't pay that much attention."

She was used to the neighborhood. She saw it every day. Sure, sometimes litter collected in the gutters. And the lawns weren't exactly fine-trimmed. Some of them were barely lawns. But the MacAfees next door were a lovely retired couple, and Sage's landlord, Hank Taylor, owned the bakery two blocks down. He was a hardworking, fiftysomething man who looked out for her and Eli.

TJ opened his door and got out, staring levelly at the group of boys.

Sage followed and got out her side.

"Ignore them," she told TJ.

"They're trying to decide if they can intimidate me."

"If you don't bother them, they won't bother you."

"I don't want them to bother my car."

"Don't be paranoid." She started across the sidewalk for the worn stepping stones that led to the basement entrance.

"How long have you lived here?" he asked, falling into step.

"Since Eli was two."

"Has it always been like this?" His tone was clearly critical.

"You mean low-rent?"

"This is a little more than low-rent."

She inserted her key into the doorknob and turned it open.

"No dead bolt?" he asked.

"It's not exactly a high crime district."

"Could have fooled me."

Insulted and annoyed, she stepped into the doorway and turned. "Thanks for the ride, TJ."

He looked confused. "You don't want to talk?"

"About?"

"About our situation." His gaze took in the room behind her.

It was clean. Maybe a little cluttered, since she'd spent so much time at the hospital the past two weeks. There were dishes in the drainer and a basket of clean laundry on the sofa. She'd been to the Laundromat but hadn't had time to put everything away.

She realized he had to be used to far more opulent surroundings, but she wasn't going to apologize. She had a limited budget. Eli had a safe, clean place to live. His school was basic, but the teachers were dedicated. And the park down the street was part of a city beautification project and was a perfectly nice place for him to play.

"I'm tired," she said to TJ. "Can we talk tomorrow?"

He glanced at his watch. "I really don't want to leave you here alone."

"It's my home. You're being both ridiculous and insulting."

She'd been aware of the neighborhood slipping in recent years. But it was still a perfectly fine place to live.

"There are thugs on the front sidewalk."

"Those are kids."

"Those *kids* have been shaving for more than a few years. They could be armed."

She'd had enough. "Good night, TJ. Go back to your five-star hotel. Eat some twenty-dollar almonds from the minibar or something."

"Come with me," he said.

In exasperation, she dropped her purse on the bookshelf. "I'm sleeping in my own bed tonight. Just like I did last night and just like I'll be doing tomorrow night."

He opened his mouth.

"Stop," she ordered. She pointed out the door. "Go. I'll meet you at the hospital tomorrow."

"I'll pick you up."

"No, you won't. I already regret letting you drive me home."

"No, you don't."

He was right. She didn't. If he hadn't driven her home, she'd still be standing at the downtown station.

"Why are you fighting me on this?" he asked.

It was a fair question. She wasn't exactly sure. "I think mostly because you're overbearing."

"I'm logical and reasonable."

His answer surprised a laugh out of her. "Is that how you see yourself?"

"I'm staying at the Bayside Hotel."

"Are you bragging?"

He gave an exaggerated sigh. "I'm pointing out my geographic location. It's downtown. It's not even out of my way to pick you up tomorrow." Before she could respond, he continued. "Logic and reason."

"And a little bit overbearing."

"Only a little bit. Eight?"

She didn't want to give in. It felt too much like giving up. "TJ…"

"Eight it is." He gave her shoulder an unexpected squeeze. "Lock the door behind me."

And then he was gone. And her shoulder tingled from his touch. And she wanted to be annoyed with him. But her heart wasn't in it.

Eli seemed to rally in the morning but then faded in the afternoon. The nurses assured them it was normal. TJ made himself scarce for a while to give Sage time alone with Eli, returning to his hotel to touch base with his executive assistant.

While he followed up with the most pressing phone calls, he couldn't get Sage and Eli's apartment off his mind. He understood that it was hard being a single mother. His own mother had struggled to raise him and his two brothers. There was no shame in financial hardship, especially when a woman was juggling both work and parenting.

But Sage didn't need to struggle anymore. She didn't need to worry about money anymore.

He wanted them out of that neighborhood. What was more, he wanted Eli in Whiskey Bay. He might not be feeling quite as hard-nosed about it after the past few days with Sage. But he was still determined to be part of Eli's day-to-day life from here on in.

He didn't know how he'd pull it off, but he knew it would go a lot smoother if he could convince Sage instead of fighting her. As quickly as the thought formed, it also crystallized. If he wanted to win over Sage, he had to show her the possibilities. To show her the possibilities, he had to show her Whiskey Bay.

Back in the hospital, Eli was still feeling low. He barely touched his dinner. And by six he was sound asleep.

"Tomorrow will be better," TJ said to Sage as she kissed Eli's forehead.

"He feels warm." She drew back and cupped her hand on his head.

"The nurse just took his temperature."

"We should ask her to recheck it."

TJ put a hand on Sage's slim shoulder. "They will. They'll monitor it all night."

"What if he gets a fever?"

"You're borrowing trouble." TJ hated to see her stressing herself out. It wasn't going to change the outcome. "We should get something to eat."

"I'd rather stay here."

"There's nothing you can do while he sleeps."

Sage took Eli's hand. "I know."

"There are absolutely no warning signs." TJ wanted to take Sage's hand. "It's simply going to be a long road to recovery."

"I'm telling myself the same thing."

He moved so he was looking at her. "The best thing, the very best thing you can do for Eli is stay strong and healthy yourself."

She gave a ghost of a smile. "Stop being right."

"I can't help it."

Her smile went wider.

He was encouraged. "Let's go get a nice dinner. You've got the nurses' station on speed dial."

She arched a brow. "Are you mocking me?"

"No, I'm trying to cheer you up. He's doing great. You can afford to think positively."

She lifted Eli's hand and gave it a light kiss. "I don't want to jinx it."

"You can't jinx it. There is no jinx it. Your IQ is in the stratosphere. You know worrying yourself sick will have absolutely no beneficial effect on Eli's health."

She looked like she wanted to argue.

"You got straight As in science."

She'd gotten straight As in everything.

"It's true that I'm not superstitious," she said. Her shoulders relaxed.

"I have a very nice restaurant in mind." He had no intention of telling her the details, at least not until he had to.

"Okay. You're right. Dinner would be nice."

"Can you say that again?" he teased.

"Dinner would be nice." She smirked at him.

"I do like being right."

"You have an ego, TJ." She rose from the edge of the bed and gathered her purse.

It was clear she was mocking him, but she could be right.

He definitely liked to accomplish things. It felt good to succeed. And he liked to be the best he could.

When he discovered he was falling behind in something, he took immediate steps to catch up. Take last year. He'd discovered he was getting out of shape, that both Matt and Caleb could outrun him.

He'd hit the gym, started rowing and biking. He could now beat both of them in a five-mile run. He hadn't thought about why it mattered to him. But ego would definitely explain it.

"Seafood okay with you?" he asked as they made their way toward the parking lot.

"Anything's okay with me. But I can't let you keep paying."

He almost laughed at that. "I've got a lot of paying to make up for."

"With Eli, sure. But not with me. You don't owe me anything."

"Other than nine years of child support?"

"I'm not asking for that." Her tone was genuinely horrified. "I'd never ask for that. None of this has anything to do with money."

"I know it doesn't." How could he not know that?

The fact that he'd found out about Eli at all was a bizarre coincidence. His anger still simmered when he thought about her secrecy. But now wasn't the time to rehash her past decisions. The last thing he wanted to do was fight.

"I won't take your money," she said.

"It's dinner, Sage. I'm buying you dinner. People do that with their friends every day."

"We're not friends."

"Well, I hope we're going to be friends. Things are going to be a whole lot easier if we're friendly."

She didn't seem to have a response for that, and they'd arrived at his car.

"Are you afraid of flying?" he asked as they got inside.

"No," she said. "I mean, it's not something I do. We're hardly in a position to take sun vacations. But I'm not afraid of it." Her tone turned suspicious. "Why? Why are you asking? Are you looking for genetic flaws?"

"Genetic... *No*."

"I doubt irrational fears are inherited, anyway."

"I'm not looking for genetic flaws. You *have* no genetic flaws." He pulled onto the street.

"I have red hair and freckles."

"The freckles have faded." He'd always thought they were cute. "And your hair's not red, it's auburn. It's a beautiful shade of auburn. Do you know how much women pay to get that color hair? And you're absolutely brilliant. What is your IQ, anyway?"

"I'm not telling you my IQ."

"That high, huh?"

"No, it's not that high. It's not anywhere near..." She blew out what sounded like a tired sigh.

He let it lie as they zipped through the light traffic.

Twelve blocks later he flipped on his signal and pulled up to the Brandywine Hotel.

"Are we eating here?" she asked, glancing around at the brick-lined drive and the lighted gardens.

"Not exactly."

He exited the car and came around to her door.

"We're walking?" she asked as she stepped out.

The valet arrived, and TJ handed him the keys, giving the uniformed man his name.

"Not exactly," TJ answered Sage, gesturing to the revolving glass door.

"I don't understand."

"There's a helipad on the top of the hotel."

"A what?" She looked straight up the outside of the building. "There's a restaurant up there?"

"No." He let her go first through the door. "That's not a euphemism. I mean a helipad, a place where helicopters can land and take off."

"Why?" She looked perplexed.

"You said you weren't afraid to fly."

"You said we were going for dinner."

"We are."

She gave him a look that questioned his intellect. "In a helicopter? Are you showing off?"

"No. I'm being practical." He touched the elevator button.

"This, I have got to hear."

"We're going to the Crab Shack. It's a great little seafood restaurant."

"By *helicopter*?"

"It's faster."

"Faster than what?"

"Than a car."

The door closed behind him. He inserted a key card and pressed the button for the rooftop.

She watched his motions. "Do you have a room here?"

He glanced at the card before putting it back in his

pocket. "No. I made arrangements earlier to access the helipad."

"You planned this?"

"Yes, I planned this. Helicopters don't just swoop in for me on a moment's notice."

She was silent as the floors pinged by.

"Is this place fancy?" she asked.

"You look fine. You look better than fine."

"Is it fancy?"

"Not really. It's pretty down-to-earth."

"Is it on an island? Do we have to cross the strait?"

As the door slid open, TJ turned his head from her and mumbled, "It's in Whiskey Bay."

"What did you say?"

He gave up the subterfuge. "I said it's in Whiskey Bay."

She stopped dead, her eyes going round as she stared at him. "What are you doing, TJ?"

"You might as well see the community."

"Are you kidnapping me?"

"Of course not."

Her gaze slid to the helicopter. "And if I don't want to get onboard?"

"Then you'll miss the ride of your life, a great seafood dinner and a chance to see where I live."

Four

TJ had been right. The seafood dinner at the Crab Shack was terrific, and the helicopter ride had been the adventure of Sage's life. It took only thirty minutes, and it was smoother than she'd expected. The altitude was low, and her view of the lights on the ground and the stars above had been amazing.

When they'd landed, she'd discovered TJ owned another vehicle. She didn't know why that had surprised her, but it had. This one was a luxurious SUV.

As they drove along the coast highway through Whiskey Bay, he explained that having all-wheel drive came in handy when he wanted to take gravel roads. He liked to mountain bike, but he didn't like taking his sports car off the pavement.

It made perfect sense the way he explained it. If you were a gazillionaire, why wouldn't you have as many vehicles as your heart desired?

"See, it's only about fifteen minutes from my place to the hospital," he said as they turned into the parking lot.

He'd pointed out his driveway, which was close to the Crab Shack.

There was no pay kiosk at this hospital. As far as she could see, parking was free. She had to admit, it was a nice perk for patients and visitors.

"I think you'll be impressed," he said as he chose a spot.

"You're not going to change my mind." She wasn't looking at the Highside Hospital to be impressed. She wanted to be in a position to advocate for St. Bea's. Halfway through dinner, she'd realized she could do that better once she'd taken a look at the competition…and discovered its flaws.

"I'm looking for a conversation, not a debate," he said.

"I don't believe that for a second."

They both climbed out of the SUV.

Both the parking lot and the entrance area were well lit. A few people entered and exited the building, some of them in uniform, some obviously visitors or patients.

The Highside Hospital sign was in stylized red lettering across the front of the building. Inside, the foyer was bright and expansive, with high ceilings and a view of some open hallways above. The colors were bolder than she'd expected. There were comfortable seating areas and a long reception counter with several available nurses, two of whom looked up and greeted them with a welcoming smile.

Before they made it to the reception desk, a slim, thirtysomething woman in a blazer and a straight skirt approached. Her brunette hair was neatly twisted into

a braid. Everything about her projected a calm profes-
sionalism.

"Mr. Bauer. It's so nice to see you here." Her voice
was friendly as she shook TJ's hand. Then she looked
expectantly in Sage's direction.

"This is a friend. Sage Costas. Sage, this is Natalie
Moreau, the assistant manager of patient care here at
Highside."

"It's very nice to meet you." Sage couldn't help but
wonder if TJ had called ahead, and she was about to get
the full court press.

It wasn't going to help him. She wasn't going to be
swayed by his connections to the bigwigs any more than
she was by the big lobby.

"I'm sorry to drop in like this," TJ said to Natalie.

Despite his words, Sage still suspected a setup.

"You're welcome anytime," Natalie told him.

"Sage has a nine-year-old son who is ill, and I was
hoping we could show her the facilities."

The concern that appeared on Natalie's face seemed
genuine. "I'm so sorry to hear that. I can show you
around right now and answer any questions you have."

"We don't mean to interrupt your evening," TJ said.
"Perhaps one of the nurses might have time to accom-
pany us—"

"Nonsense," Natalie said, her tone going brisk.
"You're not interrupting at all. Why don't we start with
the lounge and restaurant area?"

She directed her attention to Sage. "There are several visitor lounge areas on the main floor, and two
on each patient floor. There are patient lounges too, of
course. But we want visitors—especially the parents of
young children—to have some space to decompress."

She started to walk. "If you'll follow me, I can show you where we converted the cafeteria into two spaces, a full-service restaurant and a grab-and-go coffee bar. Over the past four years, we've put significant emphasis on dining options for both patients and visitors. We're particularly attuned to allergies and sensitivities. Our head chef has started several innovative programs, including using organic and local foods. We're providing better nutrition, a more enjoyable dining experience and improved outcomes all around. It's amazing how a nicely presented, delicious meal option encourages recovering patients to eat. Who could have guessed?" She gave a light laugh.

As they walked, Sage took everything in. It was impossible not to be impressed. The furniture, the construction, the fixtures, everything was good quality and top caliber. Nobody they met seemed rushed or stressed. She knew it was a hospital, but it felt more like a hotel.

They passed through a set of double doors.

"This is a typical patient room." Natalie opened a doorway. "The rooms are private, but the walls are retractable into quads. Occasionally, we have patients who prefer to be in a room with someone else, siblings after a car accident for example. The patient lounge areas provide another place for social interaction. On our pediatrics floors, there are playrooms instead."

"How do kids get to the playroom?" Sage asked.

Eli was bedridden and likely would remain that way for some time to come.

"They can walk, or use a wheelchair, or even have their beds moved for periods of time. Our staff-to-patient ratio is one of the best in the country, so there's plenty of help for patients requiring assistance. The beds are fully automated." Natalie used a remote control to demonstrate. "Each room has a fully capable entertainment and communications station."

Sage took in the wide screen on the wall and the keyboard on a rolling table. "Are you telling me patients can check their email and surf the net?"

"They can. Obviously, many people are too ill to use all the services. But as they recover, we strive to make their stay as homelike as possible."

There were two armchairs with a small table between them in a corner by the window. The colors were warm, green and copper, even the floor was a faux wood grain. There wasn't a speck of beige in sight.

Sage could see why TJ liked the place, particularly when she considered the level of service he must be used to in his life. But she still wasn't changing her mind. Eli was perfectly fine at St. Bea's. He might not have internet access, but he had his mother, and that was far more important.

"Can you talk about your oncology services?" TJ asked Natalie.

"The best, most progressive in the country." She sounded proud. "We attracted top-rated doctors and researchers. Is your son struggling with cancer?" she asked Sage.

"Leukemia," Sage answered.

Natalie touched her arm in sympathy. "Do you have a prognosis?"

"He's just had a bone marrow transplant. At St. Bea's."

"That's encouraging."

"TJ was the donor," Sage felt honor-bound to add.

Natalie smiled. "How fortunate you were to find a match."

"He's doing well so far. It's a good hospital."

"I know some of the staff there. They're very dedicated, with excellent clinical skills."

Sage gave a satisfied glance in TJ's direction.

"I'm interested in transferring him to Highside," he said.

"I'm not," Sage said.

"It's a personal decision." There was a slight rebuke for TJ in Natalie's tone.

"St. Bea's is much closer to my house," Sage said.

Natalie gestured to the hospital room door. "For all our fancy facilities, nothing replaces family."

"Thank you." For some reason, emotion welled up in Sage's throat.

"I'm not suggesting she won't see him," TJ said as they walked, the barest hint of exasperation in his tone.

"Highside is a long way from Seattle," Natalie said.

Sage was now completely convinced Natalie wasn't part of any plot to sway her.

"She can stay in the parents' residence," TJ said.

"I have a job," Sage put in.

Natalie halted. "Mr. Bauer, we love you dearly, and we are beyond grateful for your financial support—"

"This isn't about my money."

"The decision is Sage's alone. It's her son. She knows what's best for her family."

Sage struggled not to look at TJ, but she couldn't help herself.

The set of his jaw betrayed his annoyance, but it didn't look like he was going to blurt out the fact that he was Eli's father.

"Do you have any more questions?" Natalie asked Sage.

"No. Thank you so much for your time."

Natalie took both of Sage's hands. "Good luck with

your son. I hope his recovery is fast. We're here if you need us. But there's no wrong choice for you to make."

A wave of guilt passed through Sage. She liked Natalie. She liked her a lot. And she liked everything she'd seen at Highside.

But she couldn't leave Seattle, and she couldn't let TJ pull her and Eli apart. She had to believe Eli would recover equally well at St. Bea's. She had to believe it.

TJ didn't know how he'd failed. But he had. He'd counted on Natalie, or anyone else at Highside Hospital for that matter, to point out the merits of the institution and impress Sage with the level of care Eli could expect. What he hadn't counted on was for Natalie to take Sage's side.

He hadn't wanted to blurt out that he was Eli's father. That wouldn't have been fair to Sage, and he was determined that Eli would be the next person he told. But maybe that was a mistake. Maybe Natalie's attitude would have been different if she'd known that it wasn't just a mother's support at stake here, but a father's support as well.

"Can we go back to Seattle now?" Sage asked as she tucked her phone into her purse.

They were driving down the coast highway toward the Crab Shack. The helicopter was on standby in a parking lot nearby.

"Any news?" he asked, referring to the text message she had just checked.

"He's still asleep."

"That's good." TJ hoped Eli would have a restful night.

"It's getting late." She made a point of looking at her watch.

"I just need to make one stop."

"Are you kidding me?" The exasperation in her tone was clear.

"It's at my house. It's not out of our way."

"Fine," she said tersely.

"Are you angry?"

"I'm frustrated."

"You couldn't make the right decision without all the facts." It hadn't gone his way, but he still believed that. Not that he was giving up this easily.

"I'd already made the right decision."

"You're too smart to make that argument."

"Okay. I saw Highside. It's good. It's terrific. But you already know that. And I never disputed it. My argument was never that Highside wasn't a great facility. It was that *I* wasn't in Whiskey Bay."

"We can change that." They could easily change that.

"I'm not quitting my job. I'm not giving up my apartment."

"It's not much of an apartment. That's blunt. But you know it as well as I do. And you can get another job."

"Really?" She turned her body to glare at him. "I can get another job?" She snapped her fingers. "Just like that, I can get another job?"

He didn't understand her point. "Yes. There are jobs here in Whiskey Bay."

"For people like me."

"For people like anybody. What do you mean, people like you?" He flipped on his signal, taking the road that led to his and the three other properties along this stretch of the bay.

The houses belonged to Matt and Tasha, to Caleb and Jules, and to Caleb's sister-in-law Melissa and her husband, Noah.

"A single mother with no college degree?"

"There are lots of single… What do you mean no college degree?"

Sage was a bona fide genius. She could earn any college degree without breaking a sweat.

"I didn't go to college, TJ."

"What about all those scholarships?" He knew she'd had a dozen offers, everybody knew that. How could she have turned them all down?

Her tone was flat. "I've been a little busy."

"What about part-time?" Sure, he understood a baby added a complication.

"That didn't work."

"What do you mean it didn't work? What kind of an attitude is that? When it's that important, you make it work."

Her voice rose. "Spoken like a man who hasn't got a clue about taking care of a baby."

"I know there's such a thing as childcare."

"And do you know they don't give scholarships for that? I could get a full ride, sure. But I can't live in the dorm with a baby. So, I'd have to pay rent, buy food, cover day care, study in the evenings instead of reading stories and giving baths."

"And later? When he was in school?"

Surely she could have made something work at some point in the past nine years. She had a brain in a million. It was tragic to let it go to waste.

"Do you have any idea how insulting you're being?" she asked.

He pulled into his driveway and parked out front between the two garages. "Go now," he said.

She closed her eyes, shook her head and gave a long-suffering sigh.

"You're only twenty-seven. Go back to school now. Get a degree."

"Take me home, TJ."

He realized he'd pushed too far. "Come inside."

"No."

"This won't take long. And then we'll walk down to the helicopter."

At first, she didn't move. But then she unbuckled her seat belt and opened the door.

He was sorry if he'd insulted her. But he couldn't believe she'd given up on herself so easily. There were options. There were always options. There was always an alternate strategy or approach to any situation. You just had to keep looking until you found the right one.

He led the way up the short, concrete staircase and opened his front door. The light was on a motion sensor and came on automatically in the foyer. The living room in front of them was dimly lit by the pot lights above the fireplace to the right side. And the deck and lighted garden beds were visible through the glass wall on the far side of the living room.

Her steps slowed in the doorway and she gazed around in silence.

"It's big for one person," he acknowledged.

"Big?" She took a couple of steps forward. "I was going to go with *huge*."

"Yeah. I barely ever go upstairs."

"There's an upstairs?"

"The stairs are around the corner, across from the study."

"Of course they are," she said a little weakly.

"Are you thirsty?"

"We're not staying."

"Iced tea?" he asked, moving into the living room, taking the right-hand turn that led to the open-concept kitchen.

In front of the kitchen was a dining room and then a family room, where he spent much of his time. It opened onto the biggest part of the deck, where there was an outdoor kitchen and small bathroom.

He gestured to the oversize refrigerator. "I've got cold beer. Or there's always wine."

He glanced behind him, but Sage hadn't followed.

He went back to the foyer. "Come in."

She looked a little frightened. "Exactly how rich are you?"

"I don't know how to answer that question. I guess I'm to the point now where I can do pretty much whatever I want."

She took a couple of hesitant steps into the living room, taking in the furnishings. "Do you have a housekeeping staff?"

"There's someone who comes in to clean. And I have a gardening service. It's a big house," he found himself defending. "But nobody lives in."

She looked to her left, where a short hallway led to his study, his bedroom and the stairs to the second floor.

"Have a look around," he invited. "Maybe a glass of water?"

"Sure," she answered absently, wandering down the hallway.

"The wine cellar is locked, but I can open it up if you're interested."

"Water's fine."

He chuckled. He'd meant if she wanted to have a look. But he'd happily open a bottle of wine if she saw something interesting.

When he returned from the kitchen with two glasses of ice water, she was gone. He guessed she'd taken the stairs, so he followed.

"There's no furniture up here," she said, peering into one of the bedrooms.

"My wife…" He paused to gather himself. "Lauren wanted us to have several children. She expected we'd need the extra room."

"I'm sorry," Sage said. "I didn't mean to bring up painful memories."

"It's fine." He'd told Sage about Lauren while Eli had slept.

Sage gave an apologetic smile. She seemed to sense he'd rather move on, and she obliged him, glancing in each of the five upstairs bedrooms. "You could fit three of my apartments in here."

"It is roomy," he agreed.

Mostly, he ignored this floor. It was a waste of space, but there was no way he'd sell the house Lauren had designed. And despite the wasted space, he couldn't imagine having anyone live with him—except for Eli. TJ would love to have Eli live here with him.

He knew it was impossible. Though he'd stated a hard line with Matt and Caleb that night, there was no way he'd take Eli away from his mother, and no court in the land would let him do that.

Ironically, there was more than enough room up here for both Sage and Eli.

His brain took a pause. That would be perfect. It would be beyond perfect.

He turned to consider her, taking in her profile, his mind galloping along the idea.

"What exactly is your job?" he asked.

She glanced at him. "What?"

He handed her a glass of water. "What do you do in Seattle?"

"I told you, I plan events for the community center."

"Is it administrative?"

"Mostly."

"That sounds like a transferable skill."

She caught his meaning immediately. "TJ, don't."

"Don't shut the door on this, Sage. You could live here. You and Eli. There's no reason why not."

From the look on her face, he knew he'd misplayed. He'd made the suggestion way too soon.

"I mean—"

Without a word, she spun on her heel to march back down the hall.

He went after her. "I mean that's one possibility. We should talk about it. Rent would be free. The schools are fantastic." He trotted behind her down the stairs. "You could get any job you wanted, maybe part-time. You could go to college here. I'm a platinum donor, so tuition wouldn't cost anything. Not that cost matters—"

"Stop!" she shouted, pivoting on him. "Just stop it."

"I'm stopping." He'd gone too far. And he'd gone too fast.

"I'm not moving to Whiskey Bay. Yes, you have a right to visit Eli. And yes, we will work something out.

But I'm not walking away from my entire life to suit your needs."

TJ battled the sense of defeat. He didn't want to merely be a visitor in his son's life. He wanted to be there all the time, for all the little things.

He wanted to hear about Eli's day at school, throw a ball with him on summer evenings, tuck him in at night, pour his cereal in the morning and patch his cuts and scrapes. He wanted to do it all in real time, not on two weekends a month and every other Christmas.

He wanted Eli to be with him, day in, day out. But he understood that Sage wanted that too. She deserved that too. To make that happen, there had to be more for her in Whiskey Bay than free rent.

"Thank you," she said. She drew a shaky breath and headed for the front door. "We need to get back to Seattle."

He knew she was right. They weren't going to solve this tonight. He didn't know what he'd expected, but he found himself bitterly disappointed that it hadn't happened.

He followed her, feeling cheated and angry at their circumstance. Parents all over the world lived with their children. It was the normal state of things. He wasn't asking for the moon and the stars.

How were they all more deserving than him? How were they different?

Even as he framed the question, he knew the answer was patently obvious. Those parents were in love. And if they weren't in love, they stayed married anyway.

And then it hit him.

"Wait!" he called out. "Wait just a minute."

Her hand was on the doorknob, and her lips were pressed tightly together. But she waited.

"I'm not being fair," he said.

Her shoulders lowered a little bit, and she looked relieved. "No, you're not."

"I can't ask you to give up your entire life for free rent."

"No, you can't."

"There has to be more to it than that."

She tipped her head to one side, looking puzzled now.

"Marry me," he said.

She didn't react, and he wasn't sure if she'd heard the words.

He continued talking. "Share my life, my whole life."

She started to laugh. Her hand rose to her mouth, and she kept laughing.

He was vaguely insulted. "How is that funny?"

"It's not funny." She removed her hand and schooled her features, swallowing. "It's preposterous."

He'd admit it was unorthodox. "It's logical. We share a son."

"We barely know each other."

"A marriage of convenience, obviously." As he said the words, he pictured her in his bed. The vision startled him. He shook it away and pressed on. "Look at the size of this place. We can stay completely out of each other's way. You and Eli can have the entire upstairs to yourselves."

"Take me home, TJ." She looked sad and tired, really fragile and forlorn.

She also looked beautiful, and he wanted to draw her into his arms and comfort her. He wanted to hold her, and he wanted to kiss her.

"What is wrong with me?" he muttered.

"You're tired. We're both tired."

"Maybe." But he knew there was something more going on.

Exhausted as she was, Sage couldn't sleep. Because, ridiculous as they were, TJ's words kept echoing through her brain.

It was likely the worst marriage proposal in recorded history. But, no matter the complex circumstances, it was also the only one she'd ever received. He'd asked her to marry him. Nobody had ever done that before.

She sat up in bed, gazing at the glow from the street through her thin curtains, hearing the buzz and clunk of the refrigerator and the intermittent drip of the kitchen faucet. A car drove past, its headlights sweeping across the bedroom wall, flashing in the mirror.

TJ was handsome. He was buff and sexy. He was also smart and wealthy. What woman wouldn't want to marry him?

None, that was who.

She tossed off the covers and came to her feet, chilly in the faded tank top and plaid flannel boxer shorts she wore to bed. She headed to the kitchen for a drink of water.

There was no way she could marry TJ and move to Whiskey Bay—even if he did have what was probably the greatest house in the world. It wasn't an idea that was even worth considering. This wasn't 1955. People didn't get married because they had a child.

They made agreements, arrangements. They figured out logical systems that would make it work for everyone. Eli would just…

She retrieved a glass from the cupboard and turned on the faucet.

As she filled the glass, she tried to imagine what Eli would do. Take a bus back and forth between Seattle and Whiskey Bay? Then she pictured the helicopter and gave a fatalistic chuckle. Yeah, Eli's daddy wouldn't let his son ride the bus.

Eli's daddy. It was another phrase to rattle around in her head.

It wasn't that she hadn't known. She'd known all along. What she hadn't known was anything about TJ beyond the little she'd learned in high school. To say the least, he was a formidable man. He was determined. And he was strong. And he was…

She suddenly felt hot instead of cool.

Then a noise startled her. It sounded like glass smashing on the sidewalk, maybe a bottle—possibly soda but probably liquor.

It wasn't the first time it had happened. There would be a mess in the morning for her landlord, Hank, to clean up.

Her phone pinged with an incoming text.

Her first thought was the hospital, and she rushed back to the bedside, picking up the glowing screen.

It was from TJ.

Sorry was all it said.

She sat down, holding it in both hands. Sorry for what? Sorry he'd dragged her to Whiskey Bay? Sorry he'd pressured her to move there? Sorry he'd proposed? Sorry he'd behaved like a lunatic?

She typed back: It's okay. She realized all of those things were okay.

He deserved a little latitude. Okay, more than a little

latitude. She'd blindsided him with the knowledge of Eli, and since then he'd stepped up at every turn. He was desperate to forge a relationship with his son. Maybe he was grasping at straws. But at least he wasn't threatening to take her to court.

She sobered at that thought. She'd be completely outgunned if he took her to court. He could out-lawyer her a hundred to one. He could end up with joint custody. Eli could be forced to spend a whole lot of time, likely weekends, summers and holidays, in Whiskey Bay. TJ could play hardball if he chose.

Her phone rang in her hand, startling her.

It was TJ.

She accepted the call and put the phone to her ear. "Hi."

"You're awake."

"I was thirsty." There was no way she was telling him the real reason for her wakefulness.

"Me too," he said.

She found herself smiling. "I'm starting to be able to tell when you're lying."

"You caught me." There was a chuckle in his tone. "I was on a call to Australia."

The gulf between them seemed to widen. "Oh. Well. Yeah, I guess…"

"It sounds stupidly pretentious. That's why I said thirsty instead."

"If you've got business in Australia, you've got business in Australia."

"Forgive me?" he asked.

Before she could answer, another bottle smashed outside. This one was loud, much closer.

"What was that?" TJ asked.

"Glass breaking."

"Are you barefoot?"

"Not me. It was outside."

Concern ratcheted up in his voice. "What's going on? Who's out there?"

"I haven't looked out. It's probably kids. I'm sure they're making a mess."

There was a pause before he spoke. "Does that happen often?"

"Not really. Occasionally. It is Saturday night."

There was a sudden banging on her door.

"What the hell was that?" TJ demanded.

Reflexive fear shot through her and she took a step backward. "There's someone knocking on the door."

"Don't answer it."

"I'm not going to answer it." Did he think she was foolish?

"I'm coming over."

"Don't be silly. The door's locked. They'll go away."

"Are you calling the police?"

"And telling them what?" Sage couldn't imagine the police would respond to someone knocking on her door.

The banging came again, three times, slow and low-pitched like somebody was using the end of their fist.

"Calista?" called a drunken voice. "Honey, let me in."

"They have the wrong house," Sage said to TJ.

"They sure do," he answered.

"They'll give up." She hoped it was soon. She knew the door was locked, but it was still unnerving to have someone trying to get in. Using one hand, she stepped into her jeans and pulled them up. For some reason, she felt more self-confident in her clothes.

"You don't sound convinced, Sage. I'm on my way."

"TJ, no. You're fifteen minutes away."

"Ten."

"Only if you make the lights."

"Who's stopping for lights?"

"They'll be gone before you get here."

The banging came again. Sage hated to admit it, but part of her hoped TJ would ignore her protest and get over here.

"Open the door," the voice shouted.

"Let's order pizza," a second voice said.

For some reason, there being two people out there made her feel less fearful.

She moved a little closer. She considered calling out to tell them they had the wrong place. It was impossible to know if that would make things better or worse. She really didn't want them to know she was inside.

The doorknob rattled, and she backed away, staring at it.

"I'm driving now," TJ said, and she jumped at the sound of his voice.

She'd forgotten she was holding the phone to her ear.

"She changed the lock?" the second voice asked.

"Key's busted," the first voice said on a slur.

"Keys don't break."

"Should I tell them it's the wrong place?" Sage whispered to TJ.

"*No.* Do any of your rooms lock?" TJ asked.

"Just the bathroom."

"Go lock yourself in. Keep talking to me."

She wanted to argue. She didn't want to barricade herself in the bathroom. She didn't want to admit she was in genuine danger.

"I gotta… Where's the tree?" the second voice asked in clear confusion.

"What tree?"

"That big, fat… Whoa, man."

"What?"

"You got the wrong house."

Sage all but sagged in relief.

"I don't… Well, crap on that."

"They're figuring it out," she said to TJ.

"Go into the bathroom anyway."

"Is this even the right street?" the second voice asked.

Sage wanted to shout *no*. It wasn't the right street. They should go find some other street to stagger down.

"We are so wasted," the first man said.

"Two minutes out," TJ told her.

"It sounds like they're leaving."

"Are you in the bathroom?"

"I'm listening to them walk away."

Their footfalls and hollow laughter faded.

Sage realized her legs were trembling, and she backed up, sitting down on her brown armchair. A car engine sounded outside and went silent. She knew it was TJ.

"I'm here," he said into the phone.

"They're gone."

"Can you let me in?"

"Yeah. Sure." She tried to stand up. "Just give me a…" She pushed on the arm of the chair with her free hand and managed to get to her feet to cross the room.

"It's me," he said through the door.

For some reason, that final assurance meant a lot to her.

She opened the door.

"Hey," he said, his concerned gaze gentle.

"Hi."

"You okay?"

She nodded, stepping back to let him in.

He pocketed his phone and touched her shoulder. "You sure?"

"Yes. I'm good."

He smiled as he eased her phone from her ear and gingerly removed it from her hand to end the call. Then he wrapped his arms around her, enveloping her in a reassuring hug.

It felt indescribably good, and for a few moments she simply closed her eyes and leaned into his strength.

He smoothed his palm over the back of her hair. She knew she should break away, but she couldn't bring herself to do it.

"You scared me," he whispered. Then he ducked his head to press his cheek against hers.

The contact was electric. Desire raced along her skin, flushing her with heat.

He stilled, and she could hear his breath hiss out.

He was going to kiss her. She could feel it with every fiber of her being. And she was going to let him. She was going to kiss him back.

Her phone rang in his hand, startling them both.

"That's not me," he said unnecessarily. He drew back and held the screen for her to see.

Sage's heart sank. "It's the hospital."

Five

"It's an infection," Dr. Stannis said.

Eli was asleep, looking pale again. TJ hated the sight of the new yellow-colored bag hanging from his son's IV stand. It was a stark reminder of the setback.

"We caught it early," she continued. "We're treating it with antibiotics. But, as you know, we can't afford to take these things lightly."

"What can I do?" Sage asked the doctor. Her voice was hoarse and her throat worked as she swallowed. She looked almost as pale as Eli.

TJ wanted to suggest Highside again, but the last thing he would do was upset Sage. He looked to the doctor. He could see it in her eyes even before she spoke. She was genuinely worried.

Dr. Stannis touched Sage's arm. "If you can manage the cost, you might want to consider Highside."

"We can manage the cost," TJ immediately answered.

"Would it help?" Sage asked, her voice raspy and paper-dry.

"I'm not ringing alarm bells," Dr. Stannis said. "But an infection at this stage indicates a challenge. Highside has the finest equipment in the country, and their on-site laboratory is state-of-the-art." She paused. "And if things were to get worse—I'm only saying if—our intensive care unit is full."

Sage gave a gasp, and TJ wrapped an arm around her shoulders.

"I'm not expecting that," Dr. Stannis said. "But at Highside, you have more options."

"Can we safely move him?" TJ asked. He'd have an air ambulance here within the hour if that was the best course of action.

"By ambulance, yes. Moving him won't have an impact on the infection."

"I can order a helicopter," TJ said.

"Wait." Sage looked up at him with near terror in her eyes.

He turned and placed his hands gently on her shoulders, keeping his voice low and even. "One step at a time. Like the doctor said, there are no alarm bells here. This is only a precaution. But it sounds like it's a precaution worth taking."

It took her a second, but then she nodded. "Yes. Let's do it."

TJ retrieved his phone. He didn't feel the slightest bit of satisfaction in this. He'd wanted to move Eli to Whiskey Bay, but he sure didn't want it to be under these circumstances.

He had the air ambulance on speed dial, and his next

call was to Highside Hospital to alert them to Eli's arrival. Dr. Stannis contacted the oncology department to transfer Eli's case files.

There was room in the back of the helicopter for Sage to ride with Eli, and TJ sat up front with the pilot. They cruised smoothly over the landscape, following valleys to the coast. There were two nurses and a doctor on the helipad waiting to greet them, and Eli was quickly whisked inside and into a room.

Once he was settled, TJ gave in to temptation and put an arm around Sage's shoulders again, standing at Eli's bedside and gazing down.

"He woke up in the helicopter," she said.

"That seems like a good sign."

"He asked why it was so noisy."

Before TJ could respond, the doctor from the helipad, a lanky, fortysomething, dark-haired man, reentered the room.

"I'm Dr. Westray." He reached out to shake TJ's hand.

TJ shook, cocking his head toward Sage. "This is Sage Costas, Eli's mother."

The doctor turned his attention to her. He had a soothingly gentle manner. "It's good to meet you, Sage. I want to assure you Eli is getting the very best care. I've looked over his chart, and I just got off the phone with Dr. Stannis. We're optimistic we can beat this infection."

"How's he doing?" Sage asked. She reached out to smooth her hand across Eli's forehead.

"His temperature has come down a little bit. It's too soon to conclude that this particular antibiotic will defeat it. But that's a good sign. It's the best sign we can have right now."

Sage gave a shaky sigh.

"Would you like to sit down?" the doctor asked her.

TJ quickly moved a chair, and Sage sat.

"I want to stay," she said.

"You can stay with him as long as you like," Dr. Westray told her. "And we have a residence for parents connected to the hospital, so you can be close by. The nurse will request a room for you there, in case you want to get some sleep, or take a shower."

"Not yet," she said.

"I understand. We'll be monitoring his temperature and his other vitals on an ongoing basis. There's a nursing station across the hall if you have any questions."

Sage took Eli's hand in hers, her eyes shining with unshed tears. "Thank you," she said to the doctor.

"You're very welcome. I'll be on the floor all night, and I'll be in touch again."

TJ shook his hand a final time. "Thank you, Doctor."

"It's good to meet you, Mr. Bauer."

"Please, call me TJ."

Dr. Westray gave a nod. "Let me know if there's anything else."

TJ wished there was something someone could do. But right now it was all up to Eli. TJ stood by Sage's shoulder for a long while, watching their son sleep.

Eventually, he moved to one of the two armchairs in the corner. It was comfortable, and he was exhausted, and he laid his head back on the cool cushion.

Traffic whizzed by on the coastal highway, and rain tapped lightly on the window beside him. Pings and whirs sounded in the hallway, muted by the closed door.

He shut his eyes, and his mind went back to Sage's suite and the drunken men who'd shown up at her door.

She couldn't go back there, not ever. It wasn't safe for her, and it wasn't safe for Eli.

He heard whispery footsteps and opened his eyes. A nurse had entered the room. She spoke softly to Sage as she checked Eli's IV and his blood pressure. When she put the electronic thermometer to his ear, TJ held his breath.

But she smiled at the readout.

"Down a little more," she whispered to Sage.

Sage's shoulders relaxed, and she slumped a bit in the chair.

TJ came to his feet. "It looks good?" he asked the nurse in a low tone.

"Better," she said before leaving the room.

"You'll be more comfortable in an armchair," he said to Sage.

"I'm fine here."

"He's doing better. They recline almost horizontal. You might be able to sleep a little."

She glanced over her shoulder to the two chairs in the corner.

"I'll get you a blanket," he offered.

He recalled from their tour that there were blankets and pillows in the closet.

Sage nodded. "I guess I can stand to be ten feet away."

"That's the spirit."

"He does have a bit more color, doesn't he?" She slowly came to her feet.

TJ wasn't convinced there'd been a change. "He does."

"That's a good sign."

"It is. And his temperature coming down is an even better sign. Are you thirsty? Hungry?"

She thought about it for a minute. "Thirsty."

There was a mini fridge in the room, and TJ checked it while Sage sat down in one of the armchairs. He found water, juices and milk.

"Water or fruit juice?" he asked. "We have orange, cranberry or mixed berry punch."

"Orange would be good."

He cracked a bottle of orange juice and took a bottle of water for himself.

He set the juice on the table beside her, then retrieved a blanket from the closet, shaking it out and draping it over her.

She gave a small smile. "Nobody's tucked me in in a while."

He smiled back. "You need tucking?"

"This is good, just like this." She reached for the orange juice. "I was so encouraged when he drank that milkshake you got for him."

TJ eased down into the other chair. "You should be encouraged now. He's clearly a fighter, and he's almost got this latest thing beat."

"He must get that from you," she said.

TJ's chest tightened with emotion, and he had to blink against a surge of moisture. She saw some of him in Eli. The knowledge was overwhelming. TJ couldn't find the words to answer.

She took a drink. "He has your laugh. And I didn't realize it until I saw you that night in the hospital, but he has your walk. Funny, the little things that genetics do."

"He's amazing. I can't wait to get to know him."

She fell silent at that, and TJ wasn't sure what to say. There were so many things about the future they had to discuss. But she needed to rest. Hopefully, she'd sleep. Everything else would have to wait.

"Looks like you won this round," she said.

"This isn't what I wanted to happen."

"I know. And I agreed because it was the right thing to do for Eli. But we're here now, and he's going to be in this hospital for a while, and I'm going to have to quit my job."

"You don't need a job."

Money problems for her and Eli were off the table completely and forever.

"I do need a job," she said. "I need financial independence and life satisfaction."

He was about to jump in, but she kept talking.

"But my son needs me more. I'm a mom first. I have been since I got pregnant."

"I'm so sorry," TJ said. "I can't tell you how much I've regretted letting myself get talked into that stupid prank. Even before I knew all this, I've wished I could go back and change it."

She was thoughtful for a moment. "I'm not at all sorry it happened. If I had to do it over, I'd take Eli. I'd take him over anything and everything."

"You're amazing too," he said. Then he reached out and took her hand.

It felt small in his, cool, delicate. It also felt right and good. He didn't let go.

Sage awoke to the sound of Eli's voice. He was laughing. It was weak, but he was laughing.

She opened her eyes to see TJ at Eli's bedside. The two were bent over a tablet, and a nurse was standing by. The nurse's presence might have made Sage nervous, but the laugh had to be a good sign.

Eli was in profile, and TJ was in profile. They smiled

in unison, and Sage was dumbstruck by the similarities between them.

"You might want to start slow," the nurse said to Eli.

As she spoke, she put a hand on TJ's shoulder and pointed to something on the tablet screen. She was pretty, and TJ's eyes were bright when he looked at her, and Sage was struck by a wave of jealousy.

As soon as she recognized the emotion, she squelched it.

"Mom," Eli said, noticing she was awake. "They have an interactive menu. I can touch whatever I want, and it'll be delivered."

"Good morning," the nurse said cheerfully to Sage. "We have nothing but good news this morning. Eli's fever is down, and he says he's hungry."

Sage pulled off her blanket and sat the recliner up, pressing the pop-up footstool back into place. "Should he start with liquids?" she asked, coming to her feet.

She smoothed back her hair, finger-combing it. Her jeans and tank top were wrinkled. She felt frumpy compared to the crisply uniformed nurse.

She shouldn't care. And she wouldn't care.

"The menu is customized to each patient's condition," the nurse told her. "And a dietician double-checks each of the orders."

Sage moved toward Eli. "You're looking much better, honey."

"TJ said I was on a helicopter."

She couldn't help a quick glance at TJ.

He looked fresh and handsome as ever.

"You were," she told Eli. "We were worried about you."

"It was weird," he said.

TJ eased out of the way, and Sage sat down on the edge of Eli's bed.

"What was weird?" she asked.

The nurse quietly left the room.

"I remember seeing spotted elephants. And then there was a pond, but it was chocolate pudding, with marshmallows, and the marshmallows turned into plump little chicks. It wasn't like a dream. It was different."

"That is weird," Sage agreed, knowing it had to have been the fever. She couldn't help putting her hand against his forehead. It was blessedly cool.

"Does this thing have games?" Eli ran his finger across the tablet screen.

"I think you just ordered tomato juice," TJ said.

"Oops," Eli said.

TJ took the tablet. "There's a cancel button."

"Will they let me watch TV?" Eli asked, nodding to the big screen attached to the wall.

"After breakfast," Sage said.

After the words were out, she wondered why she felt like she had to restrict his television time. Who cared if he watched something while he ate breakfast?

"Do they have a sports channel?" Eli asked.

"I bet they do," TJ answered. "Your mom probably wouldn't mind if we found you a game."

"I feel like I should tell you not to overdo it," Sage said. "If you're feeling tired, I want you to nap, okay?"

"I've been napping for weeks," Eli said.

"I know. I'm so glad you're feeling better." She leaned in to kiss the top of his head.

"Do you mind if I take your mom out for breakfast?" TJ asked Eli. "I don't think we can get room service like you do."

"Do you have to go to work?" Eli asked her. "What day is this? Am I missing school?"

She wasn't sure how to begin to answer. "Did TJ tell you we left Seattle?"

Eli looked to TJ with what appeared to be amazement.

"On the helicopter," TJ said. "We're near a town called Whiskey Bay. It's south of Seattle, on the coast."

"We're at the beach?"

"Pretty close to it."

Eli looked at Sage, his brows furrowing together.

"Your teacher says you can catch up," she told him brightly. "And, no, I won't be going to work today. It's too far away."

"Are you going to stay here?" He looked worried.

"I'm staying here just as long as you are."

He seemed to relax at that, and protective instincts welled up inside her. He was still so young.

A different nurse came into the room. She was carrying a tray of milk, orange juice and red Jell-O.

"You must be Eli," she said. "I hear you're feeling hungry."

As he looked at the tray, his enthusiasm seemed to fade. "They didn't bring the ice cream."

"Don't worry," she said. "The ice cream is coming." She set the tray down on the rolling table beside the bed. "Did you see that the menu is in red, yellow and green sections?" She put her hand out, and TJ gave her the tablet.

She touched the screen and put it in front of Eli. "You have to order at least two things from the green section, one thing from the yellow section, and then you can order one thing from the red section."

"Let me guess," Eli said. "I have to eat the green and yellow stuff first?"

"That's a good guess," she said. "That's exactly how it works."

"Okay." Eli drew out the word in exaggerated resignation.

TJ took the remote control from its holder. "We were hoping for a baseball game."

"Sports stations start at three hundred," the nurse said.

He turned on the TV and browsed while Sage watched Eli eat. Three bites into the Jell-O, and he showed no signs of slowing down. She allowed herself a wave of cautious relief. His immune system was still weak, but they'd made it through the immediate danger.

A baseball game playing, TJ spoke to her in an undertone. "You need breakfast too."

She was ready to agree. She also needed a shower and some fresh clothes, which presented a problem. Everything she owned was back in Seattle, and she didn't dare put anything more on her credit card.

"I need to get back to Seattle," she said to TJ. Then she quickly turned to reassure Eli. "I just need to get a few clothes and explain to the people at work. But I'll be back."

"You don't need to leave right away," TJ said with a frown.

She wasn't about to have a debate in front of her son. "You'll be okay for now?" she asked Eli. "Don't wear yourself out. Take a nap after breakfast."

"I'm not a little kid."

"You're not. That's true." She squeezed his hand goodbye, thinking he looked both grown up and so very young at the same time.

Out in the hallway, TJ repeated, "You don't need anything from home right away."

"I need clothes." She hoped he'd be willing to provide transportation. In a pinch, she'd buy a bus ticket. Hopefully, they weren't too expensive.

"You can buy clothes in Whiskey Bay. We do have stores here."

They stepped onto the elevator.

She was embarrassed, annoyed at him for cornering her, and her retort came out more flippant than she'd intended. "I'm afraid I left my platinum card at home."

He looked confused for a moment. Then he shook his head. "Okay, we've got to get this worked out." He took his wallet from his back pocket and flipped it open to extract a credit card. "Take this for now."

She held up her palms and stepped backward. "Oh, no, no, no."

The elevator door opened to a group of four waiting in the lobby.

Even more embarrassed, she slipped out and started for the exit.

TJ quickly caught up. "Take the card, Sage."

"I'm not taking your credit card."

"I owe you nine years of child support back payments. I don't know what kind of a shopping spree you're planning, but I'm betting you can't run through it all in one day."

"You don't owe me anything."

They came to the front door, and he quickly reached to open it for her. "I owe you everything."

As she stepped onto the front sidewalk, she realized she had no idea where she was going. She stopped.

Reality came crashing down. She had no car. She had

no money. She had to quit her job. And no matter how hard she'd tried to make the best of it, she didn't want to raise Eli in a basement suite in an area that was heading downhill. He'd be a teenager soon, and the neighborhood influences would get even stronger.

TJ was the answer to all of that. He could solve everything. All she had to give up was her pride.

That was all—such a little thing. She steadied herself. She steeled herself.

For Eli, she'd do it.

"I'll do it," she said out loud.

"You'll take my credit card?"

"I'll do it all." She looked up at him as she took the plunge. "I'll move to Whiskey Bay. I'll live in your house. But I *am* paying rent. I'll get a job of some kind."

He didn't look as happy as she'd expected. In fact, he frowned.

"I've changed my mind," he said.

Sage's dejected expression told TJ he was botching things all over again.

"I mean," he corrected himself, glancing around for a quiet spot, "we need to talk about our plans."

She opened her mouth.

"Please don't say anything." He gestured to a brick pathway across the drive that he knew led to a garden. "Let's walk instead."

"I don't want to walk," she said, a wobble in her voice. "I don't want to talk. You've changed your mind, and that's fine."

"Please?" he asked.

She hesitated. But then she squared her shoulders, pursed her lips and started for the path.

He gave a silent thank-you as he followed.

"Thing is," he said, formulating his words as they made their way past a carpet of tulips and daffodils, "I'm thinking about what's in Eli's best interest."

Her tone was flat. "Is this your way of telling me you're taking me to court?"

"No. I'm not taking you to court. I mean, I hope we're not going to court." He struggled to get it right. "I have no desire to get lawyers involved."

"I don't have a lawyer."

"I have four." He stopped himself. "I'm sorry. That was supposed to be funny."

He knew he had to get on with it. He was making things worse by the second.

They'd come to a white gazebo overlooking the ocean.

"Can we sit?" he asked, gesturing to the benches inside the octagonal shelter.

She seemed resigned as she took the three stairs up. She perched on the edge of the bench.

"I'm going to start over," he said, sitting next to her, angling himself so he could see her expression. "If you could hear me out, it would be really great."

She stayed silent, giving him hope.

"I want what's best for Eli. I know you do too."

She seemed to struggle to stay silent at that.

"I think Whiskey Bay is best for Eli. I know you can't see the problems with your basement suite. And maybe it's a better neighborhood than I'm giving it credit for. And while it's true I could move to Seattle, I don't want to move. My home is here. Lauren and I designed and built that house, and I'm not ready to give it up. My best friends Caleb and Matt live on either side. I'm not trying to make it a contest. And I really don't want to sound like I'm bragging. I'm not." He took a breath, but she didn't interrupt him.

"I want Eli with me. And I know you want him with you. But I don't want you to be a boarder in my house. I don't want you to feel like a guest. I don't want you to *be* a guest. I want Eli to have a family."

Confusion grew on her face.

"You said there was no one in your life." He swallowed his emotion. "Well, I've already lost the love of my life. I've spent the past year trying, and I know I'm never going to meet anyone who'll hold a candle to Lauren. But I want Eli to have a family. I want him to have his mother and his father both and with him every day, not separate, not shuttling back and forth between us. Maybe one day he feels like tossing a ball around. Maybe he needs some manly advice. Maybe he needs a hug from his mom, a little softness in his world, the security of knowing you're right there, that the person who nurtured him since he was born is right there. Whatever it is he needs, I want him to have it."

The color had gone out of her cheeks. "TJ, we can't—"

"That's the thing. We can. We can try. If it all fell apart, if you met somebody in the future, well, if you had to leave me someday, we'd cross that bridge. But in the meantime, I want to go all in, a ring, a ceremony, a joint checking account." He took her hands in his. "I can't ask you to give up your current life without offering you a new one."

She opened her mouth. Then she closed it again.

He forced himself to wait. He'd said enough.

The seconds dragged before she spoke. "A marriage of convenience."

"Yes."

"A very radical solution to a very ordinary problem."

"There's nothing ordinary about it. And even if there is, it's unique to us. Our circumstances are unique. Why shouldn't our solution be unique?"

She seemed to be searching for counterarguments. "What would we tell people?"

"The truth. We knew each other in high school. We have a son. And we reunited and got married. That's all they need to know."

"Live a lie."

"No. I wouldn't ask you to do that. You can give the details to whoever you want. There are a few people I'd tell. But only a few."

"I can't believe we're having a serious discussion about this."

He slipped his hands from hers and leaned back against the bench. "There are a whole lot of things about the past few weeks that I can't believe."

She leaned back beside him, and they both stayed silent. The breeze rustled the trees, while the waves below splashed against the rocks.

"Before this," she finally said, "before they found you, when I got the bad news, I swore I would do anything, give anything, *endure* anything, if only Eli would get better."

TJ liked where she was going, even if he wasn't crazy about the word *endure*.

"I suppose it wouldn't be the worst thing in the world," she said.

He couldn't help but smile. "That's what a man wants to hear."

To his surprise, she smiled back. She even gave a quick laugh. "I'm not going to start sugarcoating it."

He took her hand in his, raising them both. "Is that a yes? Are we in this together?"

"Raising Eli? Getting him well?"

"Both of those things."

"You are his father."

"I am."

"Yes," she said with a nod. "We're in this together."

Six

Sage could barely repeat her vows. She swallowed again, but it didn't help. Her voice was paper-dry. She doubted the justice of the peace could even hear her.

They were in a hushed room at the Whiskey Bay courthouse surrounded by mosaic tiles and polished wood. TJ's friends Matt and Tasha had come along as witnesses. The diamond ring felt heavy on Sage's finger. She'd told TJ that an engagement ring was silly, but he'd insisted.

Matt and Tasha knew it was a marriage of convenience, and TJ was open to telling anyone else Sage wanted to tell. But for the public at large, they'd agreed it was best for Eli if their family looked as normal as possible.

She knew it was the right decision. Still, she felt like a fraud wearing a two-carat diamond.

She couldn't help but glance down at it now. The round solitaire gleamed against the gold band. It was as conventional as you could get, for a marriage that was anything but conventional.

She made it through her vows and braved a look at TJ. He was somber, almost sad. But he gave her hands a reassuring squeeze and seemed to muster up a smile.

He had to be thinking about Lauren. Sage knew how much he missed her. She could only imagine their wedding had been worlds away from this simple ceremony.

The justice of the peace asked for the wedding rings, and Matt brought them forward. TJ slipped a ring on her finger. Then she slipped one on his. And it was done.

"You may kiss the bride."

TJ's smile firmed up a little, and he tilted his head, leaning forward. Sage tipped hers, waiting for his lips.

She could do this. She knew what to expect. It wasn't like it was their first kiss. And she'd relived that one a thousand times.

She braced herself for the pleasure she remembered. She was ready.

His lips touched hers, and a deluge of emotion washed through her.

She wasn't ready!

Time must have dulled her memory.

A starburst erupted in her brain. Her skin flushed to glowing. Her toes curled, and the sizzle of passion warmed the roots of her hair.

Her lips parted. The kiss deepened. She leaned into him, and before she could stop it, she'd plastered her body against his and wrapped her arms around his neck.

TJ's hands slid to her hips. He eased her back, breaking away.

She blinked herself back to reality, mortified.

"Congratulations." Tasha's rush of enthusiasm covered the moment and she gave Sage a hug.

Matt clapped TJ on the back and shook his hand. "Congratulations, TJ."

Sage fought to bring her racing pulse under control and to pretend she hadn't just made a colossal fool of herself.

"Caleb set up the private room at Neo," Matt said. "Nothing too much, just us, them and Noah and Melissa."

"The chef at Neo is amazing," Tasha said.

"Wait, what?" Sage looked to TJ.

"We're going to celebrate," Matt said.

"It'll be low-key," Tasha said.

Highly uncomfortable, Sage looked at Tasha. "You know... I mean, you guys know this isn't really..."

"We know this isn't a conventional marriage," Tasha said. "But that doesn't mean you're not part of the family. I can't wait to meet your son." Concern came into her expression. "How's he doing?"

"Better," Sage said.

It had been more than a week now since they'd moved him to Highside Hospital. Eli was getting stronger by the day.

"He's getting impatient," she finished.

"I don't blame him," Tasha said. "Does he have any interest in mechanics? Boats or cars?"

"He's into baseball," TJ said. "He's a catcher."

"He's going to have to start slow," Sage felt compelled to warn.

The only person who seemed more impatient than Eli was TJ. The two had been bonding over sports. She knew it would be a surprise when they told Eli that TJ was his father. But she hoped it would be a happy one.

She was feeling optimistic on that front, but she didn't want to take anything for granted. They'd agreed to tell him as soon as he was released from the hospital.

"For now," Tasha said, "we're going to celebrate. This is a happy occasion." She gestured for Sage to leave the courtroom with her. "I'll drive."

"Absolutely you will," Matt said with a smile.

"He made the mistake of marrying me," Tasha called happily as they walked. "So now I own half his BMW."

"It's not so bad when she drives the boats," Matt grumbled from behind.

Tasha chuckled. "Have you met Jules?" she asked Sage.

"No. TJ's talked about Caleb and Jules. I know they have twin girls."

"Coming up on five months. They're adorable." Her hand went to her own stomach, touching the denim blue summer dress, and her face lit up with joy. "I'm four months pregnant."

"Congratulations to you," Sage said, happy for Tasha and Matt.

They started down the courthouse steps into the summer sunshine.

"Seeing Matt's reaction to the baby, his excitement," Tasha said, "well, I just want to say, I think you are—"

"A terrible person?" Sage finished, her fragile emotions careening toward a cliff.

She'd been bracing herself for the anger from TJ's friends. She hadn't expected it from Tasha just then. But she understood how they would feel.

"What? No. *No.* That's not what I meant at all." Tasha's

hand touched Sage's shoulder. "I think it's great that you're giving TJ and Eli a chance to be together."

Sage's emotions settled partly. "I know it's the best thing for Eli."

Tasha pointed to a gunmetal-gray car halfway down the block. "It is. But you count too. Come with me. Matt can ride with TJ."

Sage glanced back to the two men several feet behind them. They seemed engrossed in conversation. She expected TJ would want the support of his close friends through this.

"I'm getting a lot out of this arrangement," Sage said. She couldn't help thinking about TJ's offer to furnish the upstairs to her liking.

"You mean the money?" Tasha asked. "Money doesn't matter."

"It matters a lot when you don't have it."

Tasha turned to call over her shoulder. "I'm taking Sage. We'll meet you there."

Sage fought the temptation to look back and see TJ's reaction. He wouldn't care. Why would he care? It wasn't like he was anxious to get some time alone with his new bride.

She almost laughed at the thought.

Tasha hit the fob to unlock the car doors, and they climbed in.

Sage straightened her skirt over her bare legs. She hadn't had a lot to choose from when it came to dresses, and it was hardly a formal wedding. TJ had tried to buy her one, but she'd refused.

She'd picked up some of her clothes from home, and she'd gone with the short aqua cocktail dress bought on sale three years ago for the company Christmas party.

It had a swath of flat lace across the neckline and the capped sleeves. The waist was fitted, but the skirt was full to midthigh. It was a little loose, but it still looked fine.

"You need enough money for the basics," Tasha said as she started the engine. "But you get to diminishing returns pretty quickly. Matt's got plenty of money—most of it tied up in capital assets, of course—but he has to worry about it all the time. TJ has way too much money. He doesn't seem to know how to spend it, but he doesn't seem to know how to stop making it either."

"He's not going to get my sympathy."

Tasha laughed. "I hear you."

Traffic was light on the coast highway, and the BMW hugged the road as they zipped along above the speed limit. Tasha seemed completely comfortable and in control around the curves.

"TJ says you're a genius," Tasha said.

Sage didn't think getting straight As in high school qualified anyone for that title. "TJ doesn't know me very well."

"He says you skipped college to take care of Eli."

"I did. And I'm glad. And I wouldn't change it."

"I'm sorry." Tasha's voice went soft. "I didn't mean that to sound like a criticism."

Sage regretted her outburst. "Touchy subject. TJ has a strong opinion on it."

"Have you thought about going back?"

"Now I *know* you've been talking to TJ. Is this a setup?" Sage was only half joking.

"It's not a setup. I'm not the type to betray the sisterhood."

It was Sage's turn to apologize. "I'm sorry."

Tasha gave a careless shrug. "No need. You don't know me yet. But when you do get to know me, you'll learn that I'm a huge proponent of women undertaking any career path they want."

Sage knew that Tasha had gone against her wealthy Bostonian parents' wishes to become a marine mechanic.

"I don't know what your passion is, Sage. Maybe you don't know what it is either. But you should find it. Whatever it is, you should go after it. And don't let TJ or anyone else try to tell you what it is."

Sage was liking Tasha. And the woman had inspired her to start thinking.

Once they'd told Eli about TJ. Once she and her son were settled in Whiskey Bay. Once they got into some kind of a routine as a household. What would she do then?

"She seems pretty great," Caleb said to TJ.

They sat at one end of the rectangular table in the Neo seafood restaurant's private dining room. It was Caleb's seventeenth Neo location nationwide, and it had just opened two weeks ago.

TJ's gaze went to Sage, where Tasha was trying to tempt her with something from the dessert cart.

He'd kissed her.

He'd known he was going to kiss her. It was what a guy did at the end of a wedding ceremony. What he hadn't known was that he was going to *kiss* her—full-on, body-wide, every-emotion-and-hormone-engaged *kiss* her. His vision tunneled to her lips, and desire dug deep inside him.

He blinked himself back to reality. "She is great. I never said she wasn't great."

"But she's not Lauren."

"She's never going to be Lauren." As he said the words, TJ was overcome with guilt.

It felt like he'd betrayed Lauren by kissing Sage. Yet he'd somehow betrayed Sage by comparing her to Lauren.

He wasn't going to compare the two women. The situations were completely different.

"I'm still not sure you've thought this through," Caleb said.

"I've thought it completely through." Plus, it was done. TJ wished Caleb could be as supportive as Matt.

"Marriage is big. Marriage is huge."

TJ found his gaze drawn to Sage. He felt the rush of desire again, and he knew he had to find a way to shut it down. "It's not that kind of a marriage."

"There are no kinds."

"There are thousands of kinds. Some people marry for love. Some for money. And some for the sake of the kids."

"Usually that's when someone is pregnant, and—"

"Better late than never," TJ said. To distract himself, he picked up a clean butter knife and spun it in a circle on the white tablecloth. "I thought through the other options. I considered them all. But I want to be fair to Sage. She deserves security. Can you imagine living in someone else's house, at their whim, dependent on their good graces?"

"Are you saying you might kick her out? I don't believe that for a second."

"I'm saying she would have no way of knowing how I'd treat her. This way, the house is half hers. I couldn't kick her out if I wanted to." He kept his gaze firmly on the table. He wasn't going to look at her again and risk that emotional rabbit hole. "And I don't want to. And I never would. But now she'll never have to wonder."

"The house is one thing," Caleb said. "But the prenup better be ironclad beyond that."

TJ didn't answer. He spun the knife again.

Caleb levered forward in his chair. "You did not leave her a loophole."

"I thought you said she seemed great."

"Her seeming great and you being stupid are two totally different things."

"There's no loophole."

Caleb seemed mollified.

But TJ wasn't going to leave the misunderstanding just sitting out there on the table. "There's no prenup."

Caleb blinked. Then he blinked again.

TJ found the stare more unnerving than if Caleb had shouted.

Matt chose the moment to sit down with them. "What's going on?"

He looked from Caleb to TJ and back again, his eyes widening at their expressions.

"What?" he repeated.

Caleb spoke. "Someone drilled a hole in TJ's skull and extracted half of his brain."

"That was colorful," Matt said.

"She's the mother of my child," TJ said to Caleb.

"Who you hadn't seen for nine years. You don't know anything about her. This could be... This could be... It could be *anything*."

"You think it's a setup? You think making me a bone marrow donor could be part of some complex Machiavellian plot to steal my money?"

"Ahh," Matt said. "The prenup. I told you he'd react like this."

"It's not up to him to react like anything," TJ told Matt.

Caleb's voice rose. "How could you be so boneheadedly cavalier? Did you learn nothing from Matt's divorce?"

"How did I get thrown in the middle of this?" Matt asked.

"You're a cautionary tale," Caleb said flatly.

"Sage is not Diana," TJ said. Sage was absolutely nothing like Matt's materialistic ex-wife.

"How do you know that? You barely know her. A prenup is the absolute baseline—"

"Hey!" Jules shouted above them.

TJ suddenly realized how loud their voices had become. He looked up to see Sage and everyone else staring at them. She was holding an untouched slice of cheesecake on a small china plate, and she looked mortified.

TJ came to his feet.

"Sage…" Caleb began, regret ringing in his tone.

"I'm…" She quickly set the cheesecake down on the table. "Thank you all so much. It's been a big day. And I'm tired." She whisked her small purse from where she'd hung it on the back of a chair. "I'll say good-night."

She started for the door, and TJ went after her.

From the corner of his eye, he saw Caleb get up as well. Then he saw Jules stop him.

TJ didn't call out Sage's name as she made her way through the public restaurant. He kept a distance between them as she went down the curved stairs. He waited until she had gone out through the double doors before stepping up to her side.

"Sage, I'm so sorry."

She shook her head as she walked, chin held high. "You didn't do anything."

"I know it was Caleb. But that was absolutely the wrong place for me to argue with him there, like that, at our wedding."

"I didn't expect drama," she said.

"Neither did I." TJ didn't know what he'd expected. He sure hadn't expected their kiss. "I'm parked under the light." He pointed to his car.

She stopped. There was a note of surprise in her voice. "I guess I'm going home with you."

"That was the plan."

"This seemed a lot easier in theory."

He didn't know how to respond. Did she regret marrying him? He couldn't help but wonder how she'd felt about their kiss. Did she remember their last kiss? Had she been reminded, like him, of why Eli had come into being?

She walked to his car.

They both climbed in and buckled up.

"He's not wrong, you know," she said.

"Who?"

"Caleb. It hadn't occurred to me. But you have all this money. You do need a prenup."

He looked sideways at her. Was that where her head was going? They'd kissed hard enough to rock the world, and she was focused on the prenup?

He jammed into first gear. "You think I want to protect myself against you?"

Abruptly releasing the clutch, he pulled out of the parking lot, heading for the short, steep road that led to his house on the cliffside above. He never imagined himself having this argument.

"It's only logical, TJ. We don't know where this is going, what might happen."

She was right about that. But he was crystal clear on the prenup.

"Eli's my son, Sage. You're his mother, and now you're my wife. You two are my family."

"Only in the most tangential way."

"No. In the most fundamental way possible. Whatever happens, whatever the future brings, whatever money I make or don't make, I do it on behalf of all of us. That's what it means." He pointed back and forth between them. "That's what this means. When I said we were in this together, that's exactly what I meant."

She'd turned sideways in her seat, and now she was gazing at him in silence.

He turned into the driveway and cut the engine before facing her, bracing himself for whatever she threw out on the table.

"I don't understand you," she said, surprising him with her mild tone. "I could take you for, what, half a gazillion dollars?"

"A gazillion's not a real number."

"And you're sitting there making jokes."

"Are you going to take me for half a gazillion dollars?" he asked, knowing the answer.

"I'd never do that."

"I know."

She shook her head, and she gave a crooked smile. She was so beautiful in the moonlight. From a purely objective point of view, she was one of the most uniquely beautiful women in the world. Her green eyes twinkled when she was happy. Her auburn hair shone in any kind of light. And the hint of freckles made what would have been a too classically beautiful face more relatable.

"You don't know," she said. She looked through the windshield at the house in front of them. "Neither of us knows what's going to happen next."

She was right about that.

She reached for the door handle. "This is going to be weird."

Weird was one way to put it. He caught the flash of her wedding band as she moved and felt an unexpected jolt of loyalty and dedication. Weird or not, he now had a family. And he had a new purpose.

Sage felt like a guest in TJ's house. No, more than that, she felt like she was living in the show home in a glossy magazine.

A housekeeper, Verena Hofstead, arrived every morning. She was perfectly friendly and perfectly professional. She dusted surfaces that had no dust and vacuumed carpets that nobody had walked on.

TJ had told Sage there was a cook available whenever they needed one. He ate out a lot and didn't usually make himself complex meals, so he didn't use the cook often. But he'd left the number for Sage just in case.

Sage couldn't imagine calling up a cook to toast her a bagel in the morning or bake her some chicken for dinner. It all seemed surreal.

TJ had given her the keys to the SUV and told her to go into Olympia and buy herself a car. He'd also told her to pick out furniture for the upstairs, suggesting she might want to turn one of the bedrooms into a sitting room. She was trying, but she couldn't wrap her head around so much high-priced shopping.

For now, she was wandering through the enormous kitchen, opening cupboards, trying to familiarize herself with where everything was kept. Verena was down the hall in a main-floor laundry. Sage tried to forget that someone else was washing her underwear.

There was a knock on the front door.

"Hello?" It was a woman's voice.

Sage closed a top cupboard containing rows of glasses.

"Hello?" she called back, cutting through the living room to the front foyer.

TJ left his doors unlocked during the day, and his neighbors seemed to have a habit of dropping by and walking in. It was a strange thing to get used to.

"It's Melissa."

"Oh, hi." Sage had met Jules's sister Melissa three days ago at the Neo dinner.

"Is this a bad time?" Melissa asked.

"It's fine."

Sage had visited Eli this morning, and she'd go back later in the day when TJ got home. For now, she was simply hanging around, trying to find a way to fit into her new life. The only alternative was shopping for the empty upstairs. And she couldn't bring herself to break the ice on that.

Melissa gazed around the high-ceilinged, brightly lit living room. "I love this place."

Sunshine streamed in from the wall of glass that opened onto the deck and overlooked the ocean. Thanks to Verena, the cherrywood furniture gleamed. The leather sofas and armchairs were comfortable and strategically placed.

There was a grouping near the glass wall, another clustered around the fireplace and an intimate setting of two recliners in an alcove.

"I feel like I'm living in a magazine," Sage said.

Melissa laughed. "I hear you. I grew up in a condo in Portland. It was nothing like this."

"Did you go through culture shock when you moved here?" Sage had seen Caleb and Jules's gorgeous home.

"Noah's rebuilt my grandfather's old house. It's nothing like this. You've seen Jules and Caleb's place, and Matt's is impressive too. But TJ wins the prize for grandeur and opulence."

"Lucky me." Sage wasn't feeling lucky. She was feeling disoriented. "Do you want to sit down? A soda or iced tea? Or, really, pretty much anything on the planet."

TJ had three refrigerators, and all were well stocked.

"Love to sit down. And anything to drink would be great."

Melissa chose a big leather armchair near the glass wall while Sage went to the butler's pantry on one side of the living room.

She chose a bottle of ginger ale and filled two glasses with ice from the dispenser. It was like living in a magic house. Everything was always at the ready.

Melissa took two wooden coasters from the holder and positioned them on the small table between the armchairs. When Sage sat, she had a panoramic view of the water. She could see the Crab Shack and Neo off to one side, and the towering cliffs that curved around the edge of the bay and gave the small cluster of houses their privacy.

"Have you heard about the Whiskey Bay Seaside Festival?"

Sage shook her head as she poured.

"We hold it every July in Lookout Park. There's music, food, a homemade boat race, costumes and a scavenger hunt for the kids, and a dance and fireworks to finish up."

"It sounds like fun."

"It is. I'm on the planning committee. So I'm here in an official capacity, for two reasons."

Sage waited.

"I'm looking for a donation, of course. TJ always donates. It's really just a matter of how much."

The question made Sage uncomfortable. Although TJ had given her access to a joint account, she didn't yet feel comfortable spending his money.

"I'd have to check with TJ on that."

"No problem. I'm going to leave this year's sponsorship information. Last year, he sponsored the main tent and the fireworks. But, more importantly, I wanted to invite you to join the planning committee."

Sage was surprised by the invitation.

"It's not too much work, I promise. And it's fun. And it would be a great way for you to meet some of the community members."

Sage appreciated Melissa's efforts to include her. But she couldn't help being nervous. "How would people react to me joining?"

"I expect they'll be happy for the help."

"I meant…" Sage felt like the new kid in school. "What are they all saying about me?"

"They're curious," Melissa admitted, her tone sounding genuinely sympathetic. She lifted her glass and took a sip. "The marriage happened fast, and everyone either knows or has guessed about Eli—since you and TJ knew each other in high school."

Sage couldn't help but worry about her son fitting into the new community. An illegitimate child was hardly a scandal these days, but he would be a curiosity.

"Mostly they're happy for TJ. Everyone in Whiskey Bay loved him and Lauren. They were fantastic contributors to the community and fun to be around."

Sage grew even more nervous. "It sounds like a hard act to follow."

She wondered how deep the stigma of hiding TJ's child from him would go. If TJ was such a beloved community member, people were likely to take his side, likely to look on Sage as the villain for depriving him of his son.

"Oh, no." Melissa looked contrite. "I didn't mean it like that. People are happy for TJ and they want to meet you and Eli. Nobody is aware…"

"That it's not a real marriage," Sage finished the sentence. She knew TJ had taken his close friends into his confidence.

"Nobody knows that it's anything other than a high school sweethearts' reunion. How you and TJ work things out in your family is nobody's business but yours."

"We weren't high school sweethearts."

"TJ told us what happened."

Sage was surprised by that. In fact, she wasn't quite sure she believed it. "What exactly did he say?"

"He admitted to Caleb and Matt that it was a prank."

Sage digested the information for a moment. "I'm surprised he did that."

"It was idiotic, and he felt terrible."

Sage felt an unexpected sense of relief that somebody else knew the truth. "It was hard to wrap my head around it, seeing the man he seems to have become and square that with the entitled jock who slept with a woman as a joke." Sage found herself ending the sentence on a bitter note.

Melissa's brow went up.

The silence stretched to uncomfortable.

"What?" Sage finally asked.

"Is that what you think happened?"

"That *is* what happened."

"Not exactly."

Sage's relief turned to annoyance. "I was there."

"But he was only supposed to kiss you. That was the extent of the prank, to dance with you and kiss you. He never planned..." Melissa paused. "According to Caleb, TJ never intended to sleep with you. And back then he never told anybody he did."

The bottom dropped out of Sage's stomach.

The entire premise of her last ten years shifted.

She struggled for words. "That's... How can it be?"

"Does he know you don't know?" Melissa asked.

Sage shook her head, then she shrugged, then she shook it again. "I don't know."

"You should make sure."

Sage knew Melissa was right. TJ was still in the wrong. He'd still done something terrible. But it wasn't anywhere near as terrible as she'd thought.

Melissa gave a final squeeze and let go of her hand. "Now, the Seaside Festival. Are you interested?"

Sage gave herself a little shake. "Yes. Sure. Thank you for thinking of me."

She was staying in Whiskey Bay. It was time to embrace that reality. She'd been inching toward forgiving TJ anyway, and this solidified it.

Seven

Back from an evening visit with Eli at the hospital, TJ had convinced Sage to join him and have a glass of wine. He'd chosen a nice vintage from the cellar and was pulling the cork at the butler's counter in the corner of the living room.

She was pacing the room, restless as she often seemed. He knew she wasn't feeling at home yet, and he wanted to do something to smooth the way. "Why don't you hire a decorator to take a look at the rooms upstairs?"

Maybe once she had her own space, she'd settle in.

"Why didn't you tell me?" she asked, pushing up the sleeves of her hunter-green cardigan sweater. She looked decidedly tense where she stood in the middle of the room.

"Tell you to hire a decorator?" He turned his attention to pouring two glasses of the richly colored Cabernet Sauvignon. "Okay, hire a decorator."

She didn't respond to his joke.

He looked back to see her frowning.

"Why didn't you tell me what happened that night?" she asked.

He lifted the glasses and moved, nodding toward the fireplace. Rain had started outside, and it would be a comfortable place to sit.

"What night?" His brain skimmed from Matt's wedding to the transplant to Eli's move to Highside Hospital.

"Prom," she said.

He stopped.

"The prank," she said.

A wave of disappointment swelled inside him. Their history was the very last thing he felt like revisiting tonight.

It had been a good day. Eli was getting better and better. And all day at his downtown office, TJ had found himself looking forward to coming home to Sage.

He started walking again, setting their glasses down on opposite sides of a small, round table between two armchairs. "You already knew about the prank."

He flipped the switch on the gas fireplace, bringing it to life.

"You know what I thought," she said.

He had a pretty good idea what she'd assumed, judging by their fight the next day.

"You let me keep thinking that," she said.

"You should sit down."

She didn't. "I'm not angry."

He didn't want to tower over her, so he sat anyway. "You sound angry."

"I'm baffled."

"It's ancient history."

"History that's followed us our entire lives. Were you supposed to sleep with me?"

He met her gaze. "No."

"Then what?"

"Meet you, dance with you, kiss you, get your number."

"And never call."

"And never call," he admitted.

"That's horrible."

He closed his eyes, swallowing his regret for the thousandth time. For him, it had been about Sage. But a dozen other girls were involved, even more when you counted the years before and the years after. He wished he'd been strong enough to speak out back then. He wished he'd given more thought to the impact their little game would have on the innocent victims.

"But not as horrible as I thought it was," Sage said, sounding more tired than angry.

He sat forward. "If I could go back…"

She moved closer. "I thought you sleeping with me was part of the prank, that you'd bragged about it to your friends. All these years, I thought the absolute worst of you."

"I tried to tell you. The next day, when I tracked you down."

"I wouldn't listen."

"And then I realized that explaining, excusing my actions, was more for me than it was for you. So I apologized and left it at that."

"And I hated you."

He reached for her left hand, touched the two rings. "You had every right to hate me."

"I might have chosen differently. If I'd known."

He wrapped her hand in his. "Now, this, *this* is why I kept quiet about it after meeting Eli. I don't want you to second-guess yourself. This is on me, Sage."

She shook her head. "I couldn't see past the anger."

He found himself drawing her closer. "You couldn't see past the selfish jerk I behaved like that night."

"I'm so sorry."

"No." He needed to be closer, so he drew her onto his knee. "It's not your fault. It's mine. I pretended it was yours because I felt so damn guilty."

She gazed into his eyes. "You stepped up. As soon as you knew, you stepped up."

She looked regretful and vulnerable. Protective instincts welled up inside him. He couldn't stop himself from touching her face, stroking her cheek, tracing his thumb along her jawline.

Her cheeks flushed and her lips parted. His body shifted to hug her, to draw her against his shoulder, to tell her it was all in the past and they were moving forward to the future. But somehow the motion turned into a kiss.

His lips brushed hers. Then they settled and parted, deepening the kiss as desire, passion and satisfaction flowed through him. His arm went around her waist, hugging her close.

An image of Lauren flashed in his mind, and guilt crashed down on him.

What was he doing?

He drew back, gaping at Sage in shock. "I shouldn't have let that happen."

She breathed deeply. Then she disentangled herself from his hold, rising from his lap.

He wanted to call her back, but he knew he didn't dare.

"We're both emotional," she said without looking at him.

She took the opposite chair and lifted her glass of wine, taking a drink.

He was definitely feeling emotional. Trouble was, he couldn't pinpoint the emotion. What on earth was he feeling?

"I don't need a decorator," she said, her tone growing crisper, more matter-of-fact. "I'll pick some things out. I'm going to Seattle tomorrow."

"You are?"

"I have some issues to clear up, some people to see."

He wanted to ask who and what, but it was her choice to tell him or not.

"And Melissa came by today." Sage kicked off her shoes and curled her feet beneath her on the armchair. It was the first thing she'd done that made her look at home. "She wants me to help with the Seaside Festival. She asked if you'd donate money."

TJ would have to thank Melissa for that. It was thoughtful of her to pull Sage into the community that way.

"Did you agree to help?" he asked, reaching for his wineglass.

"I did. Will you make a donation?"

"*We'll* make a donation."

Sage seemed to need a moment to wrap her head around that. "Can I tell Melissa how much?"

He shrugged. "Donate whatever you want."

Sage stilled. "I'm in no position to make that kind of a decision."

"Sure you are. It's your money too."

"No, it's not."

He set down his glass. "You're going to have to get used to it, Sage."

She didn't argue, but her expression was mulish.

"Tide Rush Investments has a budget for philanthropic donations. It's been mostly dormant for a while because… There are reasons that don't really matter. But it's there. I'll show you how to get into the accounting system. Take a look at what's happened in the past. Get Melissa to tell you what the festival needs. Pick an amount, and call Gerry Carter. He's the chief accountant. He'll process the check."

Sage was still silent, blinking at TJ.

"You'll get the hang of it. I promise. And that platinum card I gave you? Gerry pays that bill too. But you have to take it into a store and buy something before he can pay it. Maybe a bed or a sofa, or a bike for Eli."

"This is hard," she said in a hesitant voice.

"It'll get easier. Break the ice while you're in Seattle. Buy a car or something."

She cracked a smile at that. "Buy a car with your credit card?"

"First of all, it's *your* credit card. And yes, it works on cars too."

She shook her head in resignation. Then she took what seemed like a bracing drink of the wine. "You may regret this."

"I doubt that."

After all she'd been through, all that he'd put her through, there was nothing she could purchase he'd regret. If it made her happy, she deserved it.

After lunch in Seattle with her colleagues from the community center, Sage had stopped to see Dr. Stannis and give her an update on Eli. The doctor was delighted with the news. It seemed she'd been following his case, getting reports from Highside Hospital staff. But she said there was nothing like a firsthand account.

On the way out, Sage stopped at Eli's old room to see Heidi.

"Sage!" The little girl's face lit up as Sage entered the room.

Sage smiled widely in return. "You're looking so good, Heidi." She swiftly crossed the room to give her a gentle hug. "It's so nice to see you. How are you feeling?"

"I'm getting better," Heidi beamed. "It's not a real cast anymore, see?" She pointed to her leg that was encased in a brace.

"You'll be better in no time." Sage smoothed back Heidi's hair, happy to see the color in her face and the animation in her expression.

"I got to see my mom today," Heidi said.

"That's wonderful, honey." Sage assumed that meant Heidi's mother was out of ICU.

That was such a relief. Heidi was such a sweet little girl, and her mother was all she had for family.

"I gave her a picture. I drew it of a tree with apples and oranges and pineapples."

"All on one tree?" Sage asked and settled onto the edge of Heidi's bed.

"It's called artistic expression. I learned that from a book. Nurse Amy read it to me." A cloud came over Heidi's expression.

"What is it?" Sage asked.

"Nobody has time to finish *The Brave Swan*." Heidi named the last novel Sage had been reading to them.

Sage had forgotten all about the book. She felt terrible for leaving the girl hanging.

"Do you still have the book?"

Heidi pointed to the nightstand.

"Good," Sage said, moving to the bedside chair. "Let's read some more of it now."

She read until Heidi fell asleep. As she kissed her on the forehead, she vowed to come back as soon as possible.

It was late afternoon by the time she was on her way home. At the south end of the city, she drove past a car dealership. There were several in the block, their buildings big and bright, rows of shiny new cars parked in formation out front.

She knew she wasn't going to buy one. That would be beyond wild. But she was tempted to look around. She'd never even considered buying a new car before. What would it feel like to sit in the driver's seat of something that had never been used, learn about the features, decide what she liked?

She recognized a brand TJ had recommended and, in a moment of indulgence, she turned into the parking lot. She navigated her way to the showroom, finding several parking spots out front. She didn't even make it out of the SUV before a friendly, well-dressed man approached her.

"Good afternoon, ma'am." He extended his hand.

She shut the SUV door. "Hello."

"I'm Cody Pender. How are you doing today?"

"I'm good." She was a bit surprised at his overly solicitous manner.

Then she remembered she was driving TJ's vehicle. The man obviously thought she could afford a new car. Which, she supposed, she now could.

"Are you in the market for something new?"

"I'm just looking today."

"Just looking is fine. I'm happy to show you around," he said.

"I'd appreciate that. I'm Sage."

"Hello, Sage. Are you considering a trade?" He eyed up the one-year-old SUV that was the same brand as the dealership.

"No, not trading this one in."

"Were you thinking sedan, convertible, minivan, maybe a pickup?"

She smiled. "A car. Definitely not a truck. Beyond that, I really don't know."

"I like a customer with an open mind. It's more fun that way. Let's start with the showroom. That'll give you an idea of what suits you."

Cody led the way through a pair of glass double doors. The showroom was huge, with at least a dozen cars of various sizes and colors.

"Scan the room," he told her. "Don't overthink. What's the first one that catches your eye?"

She strolled down the center aisle, looking from one car to the next. She came to a midsize blue one that looked about right.

"That one?"

"The Medix Sedan. It's a very popular choice. Great for families, good fuel economy, but still with decent acceleration." He opened the driver's door. "Go ahead and hop in."

Sage's phone rang.

"Take your time." He took a few steps away to give her privacy.

The call was from TJ.

"Hi," she answered.

"Hi, back. Are you on your way home?"

She glanced guiltily around. "I'm, uh, still in Seattle."

"Oh." He sounded surprised.

"I stopped at the hospital to see Dr. Stannis, then Heidi. I ended up reading to her for a while."

"Are you still at the hospital?"

"No…" She realized it was silly to hide what she was doing. "I stopped at a car dealership."

"Good for you." He sounded ridiculously pleased.

"I'm just looking."

"Is someone helping you?"

"Yes, they are."

"Let me talk to them."

Her gaze slid to Cody. "Why? What are you going to do?"

"Ask a couple of questions. Or do you want to talk technical?"

"I'm just looking."

"Humor me."

"Fine." She gave an exaggerated sigh.

She caught Cody's eye, and he was quick to return to her side.

"My…" Wow. She'd never said the word before. She cleared her throat. "My husband wants to talk to you."

"Absolutely." Cody took the phone. "Hello? This is Cody Pender."

He listened. Then his brow rose. Then he looked at Sage.

"Absolutely, sir."

Sage got a nervous feeling.

"I would say the LX Two or the Cadmen. We also have the Heckle V series, which is top of the line. It has an excellent safety rating."

"I'm just looking," Sage whispered.

Cody smiled brightly at her.

Whatever TJ was saying seemed to be making Cody happy.

"Yes, sir," Cody repeated. "I can show her each of them."

Then he handed the phone back to Sage.

"What did you say to him," she demanded.

"I simply apprised him of your needs."

"What does that mean?"

"That means he's going to show you some very nice automobiles. Have fun. Take some test drives."

"You're up to something."

"Yes." His tone was dry. "It's my secret plot to get you to buy a car. Wait. It's not so secret, since I've *told you all about it*."

"Are you annoyed?"

"No. I'm amused. And I'm serious. Go have fun. If you like something, call Tasha. She'll ask all the technical questions. I'm texting you her number. Don't disappoint Cody. He seems really excited."

Despite herself, Sage smiled.

Three test drives later, she fell in love with a sleek sedan. It had butter-soft leather seats that hugged her body. It handled like a dream, had terrific pickup from a stop and was smooth and quiet inside. It felt compact to drive, but the back seat was roomy enough for Eli.

She parked it back at the dealership.

"You're grinning," Cody said.

"This is an awfully nice car."

"There's another in the showroom. It has a slightly different set of features." He opened his door. "Let's take a look."

Sage knew she shouldn't be enjoying this quite so much, but she followed him inside.

"This one is midnight metallic blue, one of the feature colors for the model year." Cody opened the driver's door.

She did like the color. It had a subtle sparkle under the lights, and the hue seemed to change as she moved.

"It has upgraded wheels and tires—they're slightly larger, which is good for highway driving—heated seats in the back as well as the front, a radio and communications system upgrade—you'll get superior sound from the speakers—and the feature I like best, the panorama sunroof, which is nice for back-seat passengers."

She couldn't help thinking about Eli. "I'm afraid to ask the price."

"I'm not permitted to tell you the price."

The answer baffled Sage.

"My instructions from your husband were to find you the perfect automobile, have you call someone named Tasha and finalize the details with her. He didn't want your decision to be colored by money."

Sage was speechless. How could she choose a car without comparing prices? Price was fundamental to understanding the value.

"Do you have Tasha's number?" Cody asked.

"Yes."

"You should call her."

Sage wanted to call TJ, but she suspected it wouldn't do her any good.

"I don't usually live like this," she told Cody as she retrieved her phone. "My life is normally, well, pretty normal."

Cody gave a wide grin. "Then you should enjoy this."

"It's not normal."

"It's quite normal. People buy cars all the time."

"Without asking the price?" She doubted that.

"I'll tell Tasha the price."

Sage pressed Tasha's number. "This feels silly."

"It feels romantic and generous to me. Your husband clearly wants you to have the perfect car."

Sage digested the answer, trying to decide how she felt about a romantic gesture from TJ. Then she laughed to herself at the word *gesture*. This was a whole lot more than a gesture.

"Hi, Sage." Tasha's voice was cheerful on the phone. "TJ told me you'd be calling. Did you find something?"

"I did," Sage admitted.

"Tell me about it."

Sage stepped back to look at the car. "It's a beautiful blue, totally smooth on the road. The engine has good pep. It's easy to handle. And the seats are unbelievably comfortable. The salesman, Cody, says the one I'm looking at has larger wheels and tires. It has a panoramic sunroof." She didn't know what else to add.

"It sounds perfect. Let me talk to Cody."

"This is strange," Sage said.

Tasha laughed. "For me, it's fun. And you're going to love the car."

"It's overkill." Sage experienced a moment of serious hesitation. "Maybe I should look at something used."

"That's not going to happen. Give the phone to Cody and stop worrying."

"Okay." Sage told herself to accept the inevitable. She handed the phone to Cody.

He greeted Tasha, then paused. "It's the Heckle V series sedan with the ultra-luxury package." He paused for another moment. "Yes, she does." Then he gave Sage a smile and a thumbs-up and turned to walk away, heading into a windowed office.

She shook her head in bemusement and turned her attention back to the car. It really was amazing. She reached in to touch the steering wheel, imagining herself and Eli touring along the coast highway, the sunroof open, Eli smiling and healthy.

Her eyes unexpectedly teared up. She swallowed and slipped into the driver's seat.

If anything, the seat was even more comfortable than the one in the test car she'd driven. She tipped her head back, seeing the lights suspended from the high ceiling above. The sunroof and windows had a subtle tint, which would be nice in the sun.

"Sage?" Cody interrupted her musings.

She quickly turned. "Hi. Sorry."

"Not at all. You should get used to the feel. Tasha wants to talk to you." He handed back Sage's phone.

"Hi, Tasha."

"You're all set," Tasha said. "I negotiated a great price. They'll put temporary insurance and registration on for you so you can drive it home. All you have to do is give him your credit card."

"What?" Sage was dumbfounded. They expected her to drive it away? "What about TJ's SUV? I can't just leave it here."

"We deliver, ma'am," Cody whispered.

"They'll deliver the SUV tomorrow," Tasha said. "You can't buy a new car and not drive it home."

"To Whiskey Bay?" Sage asked Cody. Surely they didn't realize how far away TJ lived.

"Complimentary delivery anywhere in the state," Cody said. "I'm going to get a technician, and we'll get your features set up." He tapped the top of the roof and walked away.

"Are you excited?" Tasha asked.

"I'm stunned. This isn't how buying a car works." The last time, it had taken her a month to find something decent in her price range.

"It's a great car. You made a good choice. The safety rating is super high, and it holds its resale value. TJ can't wait to see it."

"You talked to him again? Does he know which one I picked?"

"He doesn't care what you picked, Sage. You're the one who'll be driving it. He wants you to be happy."

"It's a difficult adjustment to make."

"I get it," Tasha said. "Don't forget I'm a marine mechanic. Nuts and bolts are my business. And I'm firmly grounded in the real world."

Sage remembered it had been only a few weeks since Tasha married Matt. "Thanks. That helps."

"Drive safely," Tasha said.

"I will." Sage would be excruciatingly careful with what she knew had to be an exorbitantly expensive car.

Eight

TJ had agreed to give Eli minimal details while he was in the hospital. So, on the day he was finally released, a brilliantly sunny Saturday, the three of them drove to TJ's house, explaining on the way that Sage had been staying with TJ while Eli was in the hospital.

"This place is awesome," Eli said, skipping along the path that led to the front yard instead of going inside.

TJ followed.

"It's practically a ball diamond," Eli said, stopping at the corner of the house to gape at the lawn.

TJ realized how the yard could be a nine-year-old's dream. The basement was grade level on this side of the house, with a patio off the recreational room. In front of the patio and overlooking the ocean was a half-acre lawn rimmed by natural trees and flower gardens.

"We could definitely play catch out here," TJ said.

"Can you get down to the beach?"

"There's a path. It's pretty rocky on the shore, not really good for swimming. But there's a pool beside the patio. And there's an aquatic center about fifteen minutes up the highway. It has water slides."

"Sweet," Eli said, wandering out onto the lawn. He plopped down on the grass and ran his hands through it.

"That's a wonderful sight," Sage said, pausing beside TJ. "I can't believe he's finally home." She seemed to trip on the word *home*.

"We need to tell him the rest," TJ said. He was excited and anxious and impatient all at once.

"I know."

"Now?" TJ looked at her. He could see her hesitation.

"Now," she agreed. "Eli?" She walked forward.

"Have you ever seen such a big yard?" Eli asked her.

She sat down on the grass beside him, and TJ joined them.

"How many people live here?" Eli asked, gesturing to the house.

"Just us," TJ said. "Me and your mom right now, and you, of course."

Eli looked to be in awe. "You live here all by yourself?"

TJ wasn't sure how to answer.

Sage stepped in. She took Eli's hand. "There's something I need to tell you, honey."

Eli's expression turned guarded. "Is it bad? Am I sick again?"

"No. No, no, no." She squeezed his hand. "You are perfectly healthy. Everything is looking good on all the tests. This is about me. And about TJ."

Eli looked to TJ.

"We told you he was your bone marrow donor."

Eli waited.

"Well, the reason he was a match, such a good match, is he's also your father."

TJ held his breath while he waited for Eli's reaction.

It took Eli a minute to speak. "You mean, like, way back before I was born?"

"That's right. TJ is your biological father."

Eli eyed TJ with disdain, looking him up and down. "Where've you been?"

"He didn't know," Sage quickly put in.

"I didn't know," TJ said. "If I'd known, I would've been there for you, for both of you."

Eli set his jaw in a way that looked all too familiar to TJ. "How could you not know? Did you bother to find out?"

"I didn't," TJ admitted. "But I had absolutely no idea you existed."

"That was my fault," Sage said. "I should have told TJ. But I didn't trust him back then. I didn't think he'd be a good father. I honestly thought we'd be better off without him."

Eli's gaze went to the house. "Looks like he could have helped us out."

"That's true," TJ said.

"It's not fair to blame TJ," Sage said.

"It's okay to blame me," TJ said to Eli. "I'd blame me. I do blame me. But I'm so glad I found you. I'm so glad I know you now."

Eli's expression softened a bit. "I guess you did save my life."

"I'm here now for anything you need." TJ meant it with all his heart.

"There's something else," Sage said.

Eli looked at her.

"TJ and I talked about it. And, well, we both want to be close to you, as close to you as possible while you're growing up." She hesitated.

Eli subtly but distinctly angled his body toward his mother.

TJ quickly moved to finish the explanation. "After I found out, while you were recovering, well, we remembered how much we liked each other in high school. We thought it would be best, best for you, best for everyone, if we got married."

Eli blinked at that. He looked to his mom. "You're getting married?"

Sage looked to TJ, clearly uncertain.

"We got married," he said to Eli. He didn't want to leave anything out. "We want to be parents to you together."

Eli's brow furrowed. "Are you moving to Seattle?"

"We thought about that," Sage quickly put in. "But TJ has this amazing big house."

"Here?" Eli asked, glancing sharply around. "We live *here*?"

TJ couldn't tell if Eli was happy or upset.

He felt like he needed to make a sales pitch. "You can decorate your room, pick out your furniture. I've got a wide-screen TV in the basement for gaming."

"What about my friends? And I promised Heidi I'd come back and see her."

"We can go see Heidi," Sage said.

"You can bring your friends here," TJ said. "Or you can visit them in Seattle."

"I know it won't be exactly the same," Sage said. "But

I just got a new car, and we can drive up there whenever you're ready."

"I'm ready now."

She smoothed his hair. "Maybe tomorrow."

"*Maybe* tomorrow like you'll tell me *no* tomorrow? Or *maybe* tomorrow like *for sure* tomorrow?"

"For sure tomorrow," TJ said. "As long as you're feeling well enough."

Eli looked skeptically at the house. "Are the games online?"

"Sixteen gigabytes of RAM and an insanity graphics card. I'm set up for four simultaneous players."

"Are you bribing my son?" Sage asked.

"Is it working?" TJ asked Eli.

"Sixteen gig?"

"I looked into going to thirty-two, but the value wasn't there. My buddy Matt's the geek. He tells me what to buy."

The eagerness had returned to Eli's expression. "Can we go inside?"

And just like that, TJ was Eli's father. His heart swelled and his grin went wide. "Yes, we can go inside."

"A nanny?" Sage couldn't believe she was hearing correctly.

Eli was asleep. He'd chosen an oceanside bedroom in the south corner of the upstairs, with a view of the yard out one way and the Whiskey Bay cliffs out the other. The room had a reading alcove with a bay window and its own small bathroom. He was thrilled and couldn't wait to pick out his own, new bed.

"She's not a nanny," TJ responded.

They were in the family room, having loaded the

dishwasher after dinner. The views in the room were as spectacular as anywhere in the house, but the color scheme was low-key and earthy, and the furniture was super comfortable. It was becoming Sage's favorite room. She was sitting on the overstuffed corner sofa, while TJ had chosen a leather armchair.

"She's a second housekeeper," he said. "With three of us, the workload is going to increase. I can't ask Verena to do twice the work."

"I'll help. And I'll look after Eli and myself."

"You're going to want to be away sometimes."

Sage wanted to protest. She hadn't left Eli with baby-sitters in Seattle. Any errands she ran, she took him with her. And she hadn't had a social life. She didn't want to admit that to TJ, but it was the truth. Being a single mother on a budget didn't allow for socializing in the evenings.

"The Seaside Festival, for example," TJ continued. "Not all the meetings for that will be during the day. And I can't always be around in the evenings."

"I can work around Eli's schedule. I've been doing it for years."

"The point is you don't have to anymore. Freedom, Sage. Flexibility. If there's something important you want to do, you just go. And everybody's happy. Kristy starts tomorrow."

Sage didn't feel very happy. "Just like that?" She snapped her fingers for emphasis. "You found a new housekeeper in the blink of an eye?"

TJ looked puzzled. "I have a really good service."

This was too much. "I thought you said we were a partnership, that I had an equal say in decisions?"

"You do."

"But it isn't a partnership if you only consult me at

your convenience. You don't get to pick and choose. Is that what you did with Lauren?" Her tone was tart. But as soon as the words were out of her mouth, she regretted them.

His eyes cooled, and his mouth turned into a frown.

"I'm sorry." She quickly backpedaled. "That was out of line. What I meant was…" She couldn't seem to put it into words.

"What you meant was would I behave differently in a real marriage."

She wanted to dispute the statement. But it was true.

He headed for the kitchen and she rose to follow. Opening the fridge, he extracted a beer. "Real or not, our marriage is our marriage, and I'm trying to make it work. You can have veto power over this, as you have with anything to do with Eli. But then I want the same thing. I want veto power over your decisions about our son too."

Sage didn't like the sound of that. It wasn't a very workable solution. They needed to collaborate, not reverse each other at every turn.

He twisted the cap off the bottle.

She hated to capitulate. But she knew it was the right thing to do. She hated it when the right thing was at odds with what she wanted.

"We can give it a try," she said, without a whole lot of enthusiasm.

He gave a short nod.

"This is going to take a while, for us to make this work," she said.

"I know it will." He slid the beer across the counter to her. "Thirsty?"

It wasn't her favorite, but she recognized a peace offering when she saw one.

She took it. "Thanks."

He got another one for himself. "What time are you leaving for Seattle?"

She took a sip. It was a light beer, and it actually tasted pretty good on a warm evening. "I was going to play it by ear. See how Eli was feeling in the morning."

TJ nodded and seemed to consider her answer. He gave his bottle a turn on the countertop. "Mind if I come along?"

She did. She wanted Eli to herself. She wanted things to feel normal again, if only for an afternoon. But they'd just agreed to be partners. And TJ obviously wanted to be with Eli as well. And she was going to have to get used to a new normal.

"Sure," she said.

"Thank you. I appreciate that."

He moved past her, back into the family room, where he flipped a switch on the outside wall. The fieldstone gas fireplace came to life outside.

He turned back to her. "Care to sit outside?"

She nodded. Outside was a good place to clear her head. It was peaceful with the stars, the breeze and the sound of the waves.

He pulled the glass doors all the way open, connecting the family room to the deck, turning it into one giant indoor-outdoor space.

As she followed him out, she realized she was coming to love the smell of the ocean. Maple leaves rattled gently around them, and the heat from the fire swirled out to caress her legs.

She went to the rail, leaning on it, taking in the panorama of the sky, the black water, the white foam of the waves flashing under the lights from the Crab Shack and Matt's marina. Caleb's Neo restaurant was brighter in the distance. It was still open, cars in the parking lot, low lights on the patio.

TJ came up beside her. "It's so good to see him out of the hospital."

Sage relaxed. "He seemed to settle in quickly."

"You were right," TJ said. "Waiting until after he got to know me, until after he was out of the hospital, until he was stronger, that was the right thing to do."

She didn't answer. She'd gone with her instincts, because they were all she had. She was grateful it had worked out.

"I was impatient," TJ continued. "I didn't want to waste a second."

She took in his profile and saw the sadness that still lingered there. She felt a renewed shot of guilt over having kept the secret all these years. "I can understand that."

"I'm trying to hold myself back, but I want to see him run and jump and play."

She took another sip of the beer, liking the taste better and better. "You will. He will. A month from now, you'll be racing to keep up with him."

"I'll like that." TJ turned, bracing his hip on the rail. "I was going to check out the local Little League."

She knew Eli would be anxious to play baseball again. "I don't know if he'll be strong enough this year."

"He can watch. He can meet the other kids."

"I suppose he can."

"So, you're okay with me looking into it?"

Sage realized how far they had to go in getting used

to parenting together. "I'm completely okay. He's your son, and you should sign him up for baseball."

TJ grinned. Then he sobered. Then his eyes darkened as his gaze moved to her lips.

The wave of desire was becoming familiar. There was no denying her physical attraction to TJ. Just like there was no denying the danger of that attraction. They were barely comfortable around each other. Anything more than a friendship would severely complicate their situation.

"Sage." He said her name on a sigh.

She put her finger across his lips. "Don't."

He wrapped his own hand around hers, moving it from his lips as he eased forward. "You're an incredible woman."

Her chest went tight. She told herself to back away, but she felt desperate for his kiss.

"I'm incredibly ordinary," she whispered.

"Oh, no, you're not." With his free hand, he smoothed back her hair.

"This is complicated," she warned.

"I know."

He drew her into his arms, cradling her head against his shoulder. He felt so strong, so sure and confident. Years of anxiety she didn't even know she'd been fighting melted away. Eli had a father, and for the first time ever the two of them had security.

"We'll figure it out," TJ said.

She was glad he hadn't kissed her.

She was sad he hadn't kissed her.

Security was one thing, and it was vitally important to a mother. But Sage was also a woman, and TJ was a very, very sexy man.

* * *

TJ's house felt full of life. Walking in after a day at his office in Whiskey Bay, he could hear Eli chatting in the basement with a couple of other young boys. By the clacks and clatters, he guessed they were playing air hockey. Music came from upstairs, and he found himself following it.

"It's way too crowded," Sage was saying as he came to the top of the stairs. "I shouldn't have bought the second chair."

"They're so perfect as a set." It was Melissa's voice answering.

"Maybe if we put the sofa against the other wall," Sage said.

"Then you can't fit the coffee table."

TJ came to the open doorway to find the two women standing among a clutter of new furniture. "What's going on?"

"I measured," Sage said to him, her voice defensive.

"It's a tight squeeze," Melissa said.

He looked around, taking in the elements of the apparent chaos. "Please tell me you're not moving furniture yourselves."

"We're just trying something out," Sage said.

"The room's too small." He pointed out the obvious.

"The furniture's too big," she said.

"We can fix it," he said, walking inside to look at things from various angles.

"I don't want to take it all back," she moaned. "Do you know how long it took to pick this stuff out?"

"You should have let me hire a decorator." TJ reminded her of his offer, which still stood.

"I'm not ready to give up," Melissa said, giving an armchair a shove.

"Don't hurt yourself," TJ quickly told her. He could see moving it a few inches wasn't going to help the overall problem. "We should take down this wall."

Sage drew back in surprise, but Melissa smiled.

"And that one," he said, pointing to the wall that separated the bedroom from the hallway. "We can open up the two middle bedrooms and incorporate the hallway. That'll give plenty of room."

There was astonishment in Sage's voice. "Your solution is to *tear down a wall?*"

"I'll call Noah," Melissa said.

"Wait a minute." Sage held up her hand.

"What's the problem?" TJ could picture it already.

"It's a nearly new house."

"We'll still have plenty of rooms left up here. Eli's bedroom at one end, yours at the other, and the main bath and the extra bedroom on the street side."

"A sitting room in the middle will tie it together," Melissa said, putting her phone to her ear. "Noah's great at this."

"You can't just…" Sage's voice trailed off.

"Hey, honey," Melissa chirped into the phone. "Can you come by TJ's this afternoon? He's looking to renovate the second floor."

She paused for a moment.

Then she laughed. "Like you're ever really going to be finished at our house."

"Who's downstairs with Eli?" TJ asked Sage.

She looked puzzled. "You can't make a big decision this fast."

"Why not? I should have thought of it earlier. I want

you to be comfortable up here, to have your own space. You want a kitchenette?"

"No, I don't want a kitchenette."

"Noah's coming over," Melissa said, enthusiasm clear in her tone. "He's working on our house today, but that's a perennial project. He can take some time to do this instead."

TJ was glad to hear it. There was nobody he'd rather hire as a carpenter than Noah. "Who are the kids downstairs?" he asked Sage again.

"They're from the Little League team. How is this happening?" She looked helplessly around the room.

Melissa gave her shoulders a squeeze. "This is going to be great."

TJ felt a tiny spurt of jealousy. He wished he was free to touch Sage. He could still remember last week, out on the deck, the incredible feel of her wrapped in his arms. It had been so long since he'd held a woman, so long since Lauren.

He was a healthy, normal man, and he missed lovemaking. But what he truly missed was making love to Lauren, and it wasn't fair to project those feelings onto Sage just because she was here, and just because she was so beautiful.

He gave his head a little shake to clear the wayward thoughts.

Sage's cell phone rang.

"We should really get a decorator," he said. "We'll need to paint and change the carpets and the light fixtures. This is a bigger job than we'd planned."

"No kidding," Sage said as she put the phone to her ear.

TJ couldn't help but grin at her mock indignation.

"Hello?" she said into the phone, pausing. "Yes, it is."

Her expression sobered, and her posture slumped. "Oh, no."

"Eli?" TJ quickly asked.

His son had been back for a checkup and blood tests two days ago.

Sage swiftly shook her head.

"Yes, of course," she said. "I'll be there as soon as I can. Poor thing."

Melissa put a gentle hand on Sage's arm. Once again, TJ was dying to do the same thing, to touch her, to comfort her over whatever she was hearing on the phone.

"Thank you," she said, a quaver in her voice.

"What is it?" he asked as she ended the call.

"It's Heidi. Her mom just died." Sage's tone was filled with disbelief. "They'd taken her out of ICU over a week ago. I thought she was getting better. They even let Heidi see her a couple of times."

"That's terrible," Melissa said. "Were you friends with her mom?"

"I never met her," Sage said. "Heidi was already in the hospital, her mom in ICU after a car accident, when Eli was diagnosed. She's the sweetest little girl. She's asking for me." Sage looked to TJ. "I have to go to Seattle."

"Yes," he said. "Of course. I'll get us a plane."

Sage looked like she was going to protest. But she didn't. She obviously wanted to get there as quickly as she could and recognized that a plane was the way to do that.

"I'll come with you," he said.

"You don't need to."

He kept his tone gentle. "Eli should see her too, and I'll make sure you get there quickly."

"Let him help you," Melissa said.

TJ appreciated Melissa's support.

"I'm sure Heidi would like to see Eli," Sage agreed.

"Coastal West Air Charter," came a pleasant woman's voice on the phone.

"Hi. This is TJ Bauer."

"Hello, Mr. Bauer."

"I need to get from Whiskey Bay to Seattle right away. There'll be three passengers."

"Yes, sir. We have a single-engine Cessna or a twin-engine King Air."

"We'll take the King Air." TJ knew it would be faster.

"What is your ETA to the airport?"

"Thirty minutes." He raised his brow to Sage to confirm.

She gave him a nod.

"I'll get the other boys home for you," Melissa offered.

Arrangements made, TJ explained the situation to Eli and made sure he was ready for the trip.

Sage packed her son a sandwich and a drink for the flight. Despite the situation, TJ couldn't help but smile at her maternal instincts. Eli wouldn't realize it for years to come, but he had the most caring mother in the world.

The flight was smooth, and TJ had arranged for a car to pick them up in Seattle. In less than two hours, they were at Heidi's hospital room.

TJ hung back outside the door, letting Sage and Eli go in to comfort the little girl.

He could hear Heidi crying, and he watched Sage take the girl in her arms. Sage spoke to Heidi in soft tones. He couldn't hear the words. But he saw Eli take Heidi's hand and hold it. Eli smoothed her hair and spoke to her.

TJ's heart swelled with pride.

He crossed the hallway to sit down in a chair, content to wait and give the trio space.

"Mr. Bauer?" A nurse said his name.

TJ recognized her, and she was wearing a name tag. He came to his feet. "Hi, Claire. Please, call me TJ."

The nurse's gaze flicked to Heidi's room. "It was nice of Sage to come so quickly."

"I don't think anything would have stopped her. How's Heidi doing?"

"She's upset, of course. And she's frightened."

Sadly, that seemed par for the course.

"And physically?" he asked.

The question brought a small smile to Claire's face. "She's doing really well. She's ready to go home." Claire drew a breath. "We were just waiting for her mom to get stronger."

Sage appeared, and Claire turned her attention, giving Sage a quick hug. "How's Eli?"

"Amazing," Sage said.

"That's good. This is such a tragedy."

"Yes. It is."

"I have some patients," Claire said. "Can we talk later?"

"I'll be here for a while," Sage answered.

Then Claire headed silently down the hall.

Sage's gaze met TJ's, and she crossed the hall to him.

He so desperately wanted to pull her into his arms. He clenched his fists to fight the impulse.

"She's all alone," Sage said.

He nodded. "It's tragic."

"She needs help."

"Whatever she needs," TJ said. "Her medical bills, specialized care."

"Money can't fix this one." There was a shade of exasperation to Sage's tone.

He was puzzled. "Sage?"

Her hand went to her forehead. "Money's good. Money's great. And yes, paying her bills is a help."

"But...?"

Sage looked levelly into his eye. "She needs a family, TJ."

It took him a moment to get her meaning. Then it took him another moment to wrap his head around it. "You're saying..."

"She needs *me*. She's a little girl all alone in the world."

"Grandmother?" TJ asked. "Aunts, uncles?"

"There's nobody."

TJ looked past Sage to Heidi and Eli together on her bed. "You want her to stay with us?"

"I want to adopt her."

TJ had known that was what Sage meant. He looked back into her eyes, seeing compassion, sincerity and determination. "And you called me impulsive for tearing down a wall."

"I need to do this, TJ."

"No," he said, shaking his head. "*We* need to do this."

Her eyes widened, then went glassy with unshed tears. "Thank you."

She surged forward and wrapped her arms around him. "Thank you, TJ."

He hugged her close, telling himself to think about Heidi, to think about Eli, to think about Sage as a caring and capable mother. But that wasn't what he was thinking.

He was thinking about her naked, in his arms and in his bed. He told himself to let go. But his arms wouldn't cooperate. They tightened around her instead.

Nine

At the kitchen table in Melissa and Noah's house, Sage smiled at a text message from the new housekeeper, Kristy.

"Both kids are asleep," she said to Melissa, Jules and Tasha.

"Wish I could say the same about the twins." Jules looked up from her own phone. "Caleb is sending up an SOS."

"Tell him to call Matt," Tasha said, her hand going to her rounded stomach. "Matt needs the practice."

Sage grinned and typed into her phone.

"How is Heidi settling in?" Melissa asked Sage.

"It'll take some time."

It had been a week since Heidi's mother had passed away. They'd held a small memorial service, where Heidi had clung to Sage. On the recommendation of the head nurse, and with the help of TJ's lawyers, a judge had granted Sage and TJ emergency custody of Heidi. The actual adoption was going to take several months.

For now, Heidi was reeling from the loss and still struggling to heal from her injuries.

"She seems like a strong little girl," Tasha offered.

"She smiled yesterday," Sage said. "She and Eli were painting on the wall, and Eli ended up with red paint on his nose. Heidi thought it was funny."

Sage's heart had warmed at the sight.

"That paint wall is inspired," Jules said.

"It was Lauren's brainchild," Sage said, feeling like she had to give the woman credit.

One entire wall of the big recreation room in TJ's basement was designated as an art area. Once it was covered, the plan was to photograph the artwork, then paint over everything in white and start over. It was a simple concept, but the kids seemed to love it.

"I hear she had a big hand in the festival," Jules said, gazing at the large map of Lookout Park spread out in front of them. "The special lunch made with foods all harvested within a hundred miles and the local art booths were both her ideas."

Sage fought the reflexive feeling of inadequacy she seemed to experience whenever people talked about Lauren. The woman had been beloved by more than just TJ.

"Creativity is not my forte," Sage said.

"What is your forte?" Jules asked.

"She's a fantastic mom, obviously," Melissa said.

"She was a genius in high school," Tasha said.

"That's a huge exaggeration," Sage felt compelled to tell them.

"What subjects did you like?" Jules asked.

Sage thought about it. "Math, I suppose. I did well in physics. I really liked the concrete subjects. You learn the answer, and you've got the marks. The creative subjects frustrated me. How do you get one hundred percent on an essay?"

"I never got a hundred percent on anything," Melissa said.

"That just makes you human," Tasha said.

They all laughed.

"Still, math," Jules said. "I'm not exactly sure how that translates to the festival."

"I can write checks," Sage said.

"That's huge," Melissa said. "Looking at the budget, I'd say that was the best talent of all."

"The budget," Sage said, inspired. "Can I help with the budget?"

"You mean beyond your very generous contribution, actually manage the budget?"

"I'm good with spreadsheets."

"Sold," Tasha quickly said.

Jules's phone chimed and she checked the message. "Apparently, Matt's not going to cut it." She rose to her feet. "I better take off."

"I'll go with you," Tasha said. "Sage, the budget is coming your way first thing tomorrow."

"Thanks," Sage said.

Melissa laughed. "No, thank *you*. It's the least popular job for the whole festival."

"Way to talk her out of it," Tasha said.

"I'm still in," Sage said, feeling happy to be useful.

While Jules and Tasha left, Melissa rolled up the map of the park.

"Glass of wine?" Melissa asked Jules. "I didn't want to offer while Tasha was here, since she can't drink."

"I'd love one." Sage enjoyed Melissa's company.

Eli and Heidi were well looked after, and TJ had said he'd be staying late to teleconference with someone in Australia.

"Noah will be bringing you guys the upstairs plans tomorrow," Melissa said as she opened a cupboard filled with glasses.

Sage followed her into the big, bright, brand-new kitchen. She loved the hunter-green countertops, the sunshine lighting and all the wood accents. There were long banks of cupboards and what seemed like miles of usable countertops.

"I'm sure I'll like it." From what she'd seen of Melissa and Noah's partially renovated house, she very much trusted Noah's tastes.

"It's an amazing thing you're doing," Melissa said as she poured.

"I'm not doing anything. It was TJ's idea, and Noah is the one executing it."

"I meant with Heidi."

Sage mentally switched gears. "It's not altruistic. She's a wonderful little girl."

"Still, TJ said to Noah that you didn't hesitate for a second."

"Neither did he." Sage was still grateful for TJ's quick acceptance of Heidi, and of Eli too, she realized.

He could have made things difficult for her, but he'd come up with a very creative solution. Few men would have opened up their lives that way TJ had done, even for their own son, and certainly not for the woman who'd kept a secret from him all these years.

"What?" Melissa prompted, holding out a glass of white wine.

"Nothing."

"You've got an expression on your face." She gazed closely at Sage. "Are you thinking about TJ?"

"Eli and Heidi."

"You're thinking about a man."

Sage gave a nervous laugh. "Are you a mind reader?"

"I'm an expression reader. But I won't press." Melissa led the way back to the table and set the chilled bottle of wine between them while they sat.

"But I am curious," Melissa said. "Are things going okay with the two of you? There have been some huge changes in both of your lives."

"They're going fine," Sage said. "They're going good." She tried to stop a smile, but it came anyway.

"Okay, now I have to ask," Melissa said, arching forward. "Don't answer if you don't want to, but is there something romantic going on in your marriage?"

"No," Sage quickly answered. She took a bracing sip of the wine.

"Okay." Melissa sat back.

"I've kissed him," Sage admitted.

She wanted to be friends with Melissa, and being completely guarded about her personal life didn't seem like a good way to start a friendship. And they were only kisses. One of them had been at their wedding. They didn't mean a thing. Well, they didn't mean much.

"Was it a kiss or a *kiss*?" Melissa asked.

"It was a kiss," Sage said. "Okay, it was a good kiss." She slipped her fingers along the stem of the glass. "Some might call it a great kiss."

Melissa raised her glass in a mock toast.

"Am I being stupid? This isn't a romance, far from it," Sage said. "But he's a really hot guy."

"He is handsome," Melissa said. "And he's athletic and intelligent. And he's the father of your child. And you're living with him. I'd say there was something wrong with you if you weren't attracted to him."

"Well, then, there's absolutely nothing wrong with me."

Melissa chuckled. "Would it be so bad? If something were to happen between you two?"

"I don't know," Sage answered honestly. "We went into this with our eyes wide-open. It was for Eli. Neither of us was looking for a relationship, especially not TJ." Her voice went lower. "Especially not TJ."

"Lauren's gone," Melissa said softly.

"But not forgotten."

"You're two healthy adults."

"That doesn't mean we should…" Sage stopped herself, realizing where her mind was going, where it had been going a lot lately.

"It doesn't mean you shouldn't," Melissa countered.

"I'm not going to sleep with—"

"Your husband?"

"He's not…at least not in the conventional sense."

Melissa topped up their glasses. "I'm not saying you should sleep with him. Of *course* I'm not saying you should sleep with him. I'm just saying don't be too quick to write it off. If the idea comes up, I mean. Like I said, you're both healthy adults. And who else are you going to sleep with? I can't see you having an affair."

The words brought Sage up short. "I'm not going to cheat on TJ."

The idea was appalling.

Melissa's brows went up with an unspoken question. If Sage wasn't going to sleep with TJ, but she wasn't going to cheat on TJ, where did that leave her? Eli was nine years old. Heidi was only seven.

Years of celibacy stretched ominously in front of her.

The Seaside Festival was in full swing with hundreds of people, locals and tourists alike, out enjoying what had been a perfect late-August Sunday, with temperatures in the low eighties, breezes light and not a single cloud in the sky. TJ had been gratified to watch Eli participate in the kids' games this afternoon. He and the pitcher on a local Little League team won their age group's egg toss.

Heidi's leg was improving quickly, and her brace had been removed, but it would be a while before she'd be running. She'd loved the art events and spent nearly an hour wandering among the artisans' booths. TJ offered to buy her something, and she'd finally chosen a hand-painted ceramic bowl. It was brightly and cheerfully colored, and he took that as a good sign. She'd also visited the face-painting tent, coming away decorated as a black-and-white kitten. She looked adorable.

The sun had dropped behind the mountains, and the hamburger and hot dog barbecue was winding down. Both Eli and Heidi looked exhausted where they sat on a picnic table bench, Eli beside TJ and Heidi across the table beside Sage.

"I should take them home," Sage said, smoothing Heidi's braided hair and giving her a kiss on the top of the head.

"Kristy will take them." TJ pulled out his phone.

Kristy was enjoying the festival with some of her

friends, but she was on call and ready to take the kids home.

"I don't want to bother her," Sage said, rising.

"We're paying to bother her," TJ said, sending the text. "And she likes the job."

Sage obviously decided she couldn't argue with that. Kristy was a college student, and she wanted to earn as much as possible over the summer. She'd made it clear that she liked her job, and she loved the kids. There was no reason in the world for Sage to miss the dance and the fireworks tonight.

"Kristy says we can see the fireworks from the balcony," Eli said.

The first fireworks show was at eight, with a bigger show at midnight to close off the dance.

"Baths first," Sage said.

"What about my kitty face?" Heidi asked.

"It's just for the day, sweetheart," Sage said.

Heidi's expression fell.

TJ's compassion kicked in.

"The paint will smear all over your pillow," Sage said.

"I'll sleep on my back. I won't move. I promise."

Kristy arrived and seemed to take in the scene.

"What's wrong, pumpkin?" she asked Heidi.

Heidi looked up at Kristy, tears forming in her eyes. "I want to be a kitty."

"She doesn't want to wash," TJ told Kristy.

Kristy immediately produced her phone. "I'll take a picture. We'll know what it looks like, and we can put it on again tomorrow."

Heidi's face brightened.

"Or if you want," Kristy said, "we'll paint something else tomorrow instead. That way you won't get bored."

"I want to be a kitty," Heidi said with determination.

"Kitty it is," Kristy said cheerfully. "You can be a gray kitty tomorrow, or an orange kitty."

"Orange," Heidi sang out.

"Nice save," TJ murmured to Kristy.

"Come on, kids." Kristy patted Eli's shoulder, then rounded the table to take Heidi's hand.

"We won't be too late," Sage told her.

"Take your time."

"Can I have watermelon bubbles in my bath?" Heidi asked as they walked away.

Across the table, Sage gave an audible sigh.

TJ turned his attention to her. "Everything okay?"

"Hmm?" She met his gaze.

"You sighed."

"She's talking about bubbles, watermelon bath bubbles. It's such a wonderfully ordinary thing."

"She's come a long way the past few weeks."

"Thank you," Sage said to him.

"You don't have to thank me. You need to stop thanking me. I don't even know what you're thanking me for."

Sage laughed at that, and the sound of it warmed him. "Everything. Nothing. I don't even know. I just know that Eli's getting better and Heidi's settling in."

"I'm as happy about that as you are."

"I know," she said.

The strains from the band came up on the gazebo. They'd installed a temporary wooden floor on the grass and strung hundreds of tiny white lights overhead. Couples were moving toward the dance floor.

TJ couldn't have imagined his life could ever feel this rich. The house was full of sounds and clutter. Sage was fitting in with the community. Eli was making friends on the baseball team. He'd even started doing a little practice with them. And Heidi was a delicate jewel. He couldn't help but imagine how much Lauren would have loved a little girl like Heidi.

But then he reminded himself that if Lauren was here, Heidi wouldn't be here. It would be him and Lauren and possibly Eli, but even Eli would be here only part-time, because TJ would share custody with Sage. His eyes focused on her profile.

He tried to picture himself with Lauren and Eli. But the image wouldn't come. For the first time, he wondered how Lauren would have felt about Eli. Would she have loved him the way TJ did? Could she have brought another woman's son fully into her heart?

Melissa and Noah approached the table.

"Highest attendance ever," Melissa said gleefully to Sage.

"Congratulations!" Sage returned.

"To you too."

Sage waved away the praise. "I didn't do much of anything."

"The drudge work." Melissa looked to TJ. "All that thankless, behind-the-scenes financial stuff, Sage knocked it out of the park. She negotiated prices and found savings. You have her to thank for the awesome sound system."

"It was better this year." TJ had noticed that.

"Clear as a bell," Noah said.

"And her work's not done yet," Melissa said. "The rest of us can stand down after tomorrow, but Sage will have invoices coming in for the next month."

"Not a problem," Sage came back easily. "I may not be good at much, but numbers I can do."

The words surprised TJ. How could Sage sell herself so short?

"Do you want to sit down?" Sage asked Melissa.

Melissa shook her head. "We're going to dance." Then she turned her attention to TJ. "Come on, TJ, get your wife up on the dance floor. She deserves to enjoy herself."

Sage didn't look his way.

They hadn't danced in a long time, and it had the potential to be awkward.

But he was willing to risk it. He wanted to dance with Sage.

He came to his feet and held out his hand. "Let's give it a try."

"That's the spirit," Melissa sang, wrapping her hand around Noah's arm and turning him toward the dance floor. "The night is young."

Sage grinned at Melissa's exuberance. Then she met TJ's eyes, and the grin faded.

He didn't let himself second-guess. He moved around the table to snag her hand, helping her to her feet.

Sage had never danced so much in her life. They laughed through fast songs, swayed through slow songs and stopped intermittently to have a drink and look at the stars. Jules and Caleb left early to get back to the twins, but Melissa and Noah stayed, and even Tasha—while telling them she was more easily tired in her pregnancy—made it through the last song.

There was nothing left but the fireworks, and the crowd made its way to the cliff overlooking the harbor. The fireworks were being set off at the far end of the public wharf.

"This way," TJ said to her, taking her hand again as they moved to the edge of the crowd and around a set of high boulders.

They came out at a small clearing with a sweeping view.

"This is perfect," Sage said.

The noise of the crowd had faded to a murmur, blocked by the wall of rocks.

The first starburst cracked the night, eliciting oohs and aahs. It burst white, then blue, then purple in the sky above.

"Wow," Sage said, watching the flashes and tracing lines.

"Have a seat," TJ offered, gesturing to a rock ledge.

"You knew about this place?" she asked, gratefully taking the load off her feet.

Her shoes weren't particularly fancy, but her feet had been busy all day.

"I've been here a few times before." He sat down beside her on the cool, smooth rock.

The next round of fireworks shot up, three circular bursts, expanding with multicolors across the sky. Then shining streamers crisscrossed, white and purple.

They sat in silence while golden hues morphed into greens and blues.

She glanced at his profile, seeing the light reflected in his eyes. She could still feel his arms around her, the warmth of him, the strength of him. Out on the dance floor she'd been transported back ten years to another dance, another night in TJ's arms.

He seemed to sense her gaze and turned.

He smiled, and her heart expanded, tightening against the walls of her chest.

Then his smile faded. His eyes darkened, the reflection of the fireworks growing sharper, more distinct.

The bangs and pops grew muffled, the crowd's reaction fading.

TJ leaned toward her, gradually and in excruciating slow motion.

She held her breath. She closed her eyes. Her senses attuned to him.

Then his lips brushed hers and lights brighter than the fireworks flashed behind her eyes. She gasped, and his kiss deepened.

His hands drew her close. Then his arms went full around her, and he tipped his head, arching her backward with the strength of his kiss.

She hugged him tight, parting her lips, kissing him long and hard and deep. Gravity seemed to disappear, and she felt as if she was floating on the salt air, suspended in bliss.

His warm hand touched the small of her back, finding the strip of skin between her top and her slacks. She smoothed her hands up his chest, reveling in his sculpted muscles. She stroked over his shoulders, down to his bare arm, feathering her fingers beneath his T-shirt sleeve.

He broke the kiss, pulling back and staring, a look of astonishment in his eyes. She expected him to back off, but instead he reached for the hem of her top. He peeled it up slowly. She didn't stop him. She had no desire to stop him.

He took it off and dropped it to the side, then he stared for long moments at her purple lacy bra. She reached for his shirt and pulled it off, taking in the breadth of his tanned chest.

Then she stripped off her bra and fell back into his

arms, pressing her breasts against him, remembering their long-ago lovemaking, inhaling his musky scent and bringing her lips back to his for another searing kiss.

He reached under her thighs, lifting her, placing her straddled across his lap, her slacks taut against her skin, his jeans rough through the thin fabric. His fingers tunneled into her hair, and his kisses deepened.

Then he cupped her breast. She gasped with the intensity of the sensation, reflexively arching against him. Her thighs tightened around him, and her fingers dug into his bare back.

This was what had happened. This was *why* it had happened.

The fireworks going off behind her had nothing on what was happening between them.

"TJ," she whispered. "Please."

He groaned in response.

She reached for the snap of his jeans, releasing it.

But he covered her hand with his, stopping her.

She drew back. What was wrong? What could possibly be wrong?

His eyes were pitch-black. His face was flushed. And his lips were dark red with passion.

"What?" she asked.

He cocked his head sideways to the crowd.

The fireworks banged full volume behind her, and she jumped at the sound. The crowd was behind the boulders, but they weren't very far away.

"Oh," she managed to say, grateful and disappointed at the same time.

"And I'm sorry," he said, handing her clothing back to her. "You didn't sign up for this."

She wasn't a bit sorry. "No, but I—"

"We need to keep it simple." He shifted from beneath her, then he pulled his shirt back on.

She felt suddenly exposed and dressed quickly.

He came to his feet. "We should go home."

She agreed. The fireworks were still continuing, but she really didn't feel like watching anymore.

As they walked, she wanted to ask what keeping it simple meant. From where she was standing, sleeping together would be the simplest thing in the world. They were married after all, and the chemistry between them was still explosive after all these years.

"TJ," she tried as they came to the car.

"Let's leave it," he said, unlocking the doors. "Recriminations aren't going to help anything."

Recriminations were the last thing on her mind. She was thinking about what Melissa had said.

"This isn't anybody's fault."

"It's my fault." He got into the driver's seat.

The drive home was short. All the way there, Sage tried to come up with the right words, the right phrasing, a way to bring up Melissa's idea.

They pulled up to the house, and he shut off the car.

She took the plunge. "We're married," she said, looking straight ahead.

She heard him turn toward her, but she couldn't bring herself to meet his eyes.

"We're both healthy adults. I don't want to have an affair. But I don't want to be celibate." She swallowed. "You were there. You felt it too. I think we should…"

He was dead still and dead quiet.

"I think we should sleep together," she finished in a rush.

The silence was deafening.

"What I mean is—"

"I know what you mean." His tone was flat.

She looked at him then.

It was there—the pain in his eyes, the set of his jaw, the white knuckles where his hands gripped the steering wheel. It was Lauren now, and it would always be Lauren. He might as well be shouting it from the rooftop.

Sage didn't know whether to be hurt or humiliated. But she wasn't sticking around to figure it out. She hopped from the car, went into the house and straight upstairs.

Ten

When the front door had closed behind Sage last night, TJ sat still for a very long time, his feelings running rampant—a sexual relationship with Sage, sleeping with Sage, making love with Sage. He could picture it so clearly in his mind, and in that moment, he'd desperately wanted to say yes.

But that would have been unfair to both of them, to all of them. He knew he'd done the right thing last night, and he still knew that today.

He'd left early this morning, not even bothering with coffee. He headed straight to his office in the small downtown area of Whiskey Bay. Tide Rush Investments owned the building, but they used only the top two floors. The first floor housed retail space, a jewelry store, a clothing store with local designs and an art gallery. A law firm rented the second floor, while fifteen of TJ's investment managers and their staff took up the rest.

He had other branches, New York, London, Sydney and Singapore. And they were looking at Mumbai. Right now, scanning the proposal for that new branch, he thought what the heck? Why not expand yet again? It seemed there were endless opportunities all around the world. There were days when he wondered if he could stop the money train even if he tried.

Matt appeared at the door of his office, a cup of take-out coffee in each hand. "You're here early."

"I'm looking at Mumbai." TJ didn't feel like explaining his emotional state. Not that he was in an emotional state. He was just confused. No, not confused, disappointed.

He was disappointed that what he wanted wasn't the right thing to do.

Matt crossed the room, holding out one of the cups of coffee.

TJ gratefully accepted it. He'd come in so early that the coffee shop down the street hadn't even opened yet.

Matt sat down in one of two leather guest chairs in front of TJ's desk. It was a pretentious office. Comfortable, but designed to show high net worth investors that Tide Rush Investments was successful, a place where they could park their money with complete confidence.

"What's in Mumbai?" Matt asked.

"Nothing yet. Probably a branch office." TJ looked at the numbers one more time. "Yeah, a branch office." He stroked his signature across the bottom of the page.

"What was that?" Matt asked.

TJ looked up. "What do you mean?"

"How much money did you commit with that stroke of a pen?"

"Fifty million. That'll get things started."

Matt chuckled and shook his head. "I can't even wrap my head around amounts like that."

"Mostly they're just numbers on a page." TJ was feeling particularly disconnected today. "As long as they stay black, it's all good."

"And do they stay black?"

"They always stay black. I sometimes wonder why more people don't do this." TJ peeled the lid from the coffee cup. He hated drinking through those little slits.

"More people can't do this," Matt said. "You're a savant."

It was TJ's turn to laugh. "I wish it was harder, more complicated. Maybe then I'd feel better about earning so much."

"It is harder and more complicated. You just don't see it."

TJ leaned back in his chair and took a satisfying sip.

"I brought you a check," Matt said, dropping an envelope onto TJ's desk.

"I told you there was no rush." Tide Rush Investments had fronted the money for Matt's yacht purchases after a catastrophic fire at his marina.

"It's just the first installment."

"Thanks."

There was a silent pause.

"You have a good time last night?" Matt asked.

"Sure," TJ answered easily, focusing hard on the festival events and not what had happened in his driveway afterward. "You?"

"It was great. Tasha said it was the highest attendance ever."

"Good to hear. The kids had a great time."

Matt smiled. "Heidi is adorable."

TJ returned the smile. "She is that."

It was amazing how quickly he'd grown to love Heidi. Not to mention Eli. TJ's son was smart and reliable, energetic and growing stronger by the day. TJ's pride in him grew by leaps and bounds.

"Did a lot of dancing," Matt ventured.

TJ's radar went up. "Everyone did."

"Not everyone danced with Sage."

"Not everyone is married to Sage." As he said the words, TJ's mind moved involuntarily to her offer.

She was his wife. And she'd offered a physical relationship. And he'd turned her down. He *had* done the right thing, hadn't he?

"How's that going?" Matt asked. "The being married thing."

TJ stared at his friend. "Are you getting at something?"

"I'm curious. I know what you did. I get why you did it. And, honestly, I admire you for it. But I saw how you looked at her last night."

"I didn't look at her last night." As the words came out, TJ realized how ridiculous he sounded. "You know what I mean."

"You did."

"We were dancing. So yes, I looked at her."

"You're attracted to her."

"You're out of line."

"I'm just saying…"

TJ came to his feet. "What are you just saying?"

Matt stood too. "I guess I'm saying give it a chance. I saw you smile last night. You looked happy, happier than I've seen you...since..."

"I'm not happy." TJ wasn't happy this particular moment.

Matt was suggesting TJ had moved on from Lauren. That was wrong. Sage might be an incredible woman, and Eli and Heidi might be great kids, and TJ was determined to do right by all three of them. But they weren't Lauren's replacement. TJ wasn't moving on to a fairytale ending without her. What kind of a man would do that?

Matt held up his hands in surrender. "Okay. But if you ever want to talk."

"There's nothing to talk about."

"Yeah, right." Matt's sarcastic edge obviously came from knowing TJ for years and years.

"She's sexy, okay?" TJ blurted out.

"No kidding."

TJ shot him a glare.

"From an objective point of view," Matt said. "Hey, I'm married. And Tasha's sexier than any woman in the world."

TJ disagreed with that. "She's..." He struggled to put his perception into words. "Her smile, and the way she moves. When she laughs, and you should see her playing with the kids."

A memory of a game of Frisbee came into his mind, Sage leaping in the air and sprinting across the grass, barefoot, laughing, her toned, tanned legs in the bright sunshine.

"It would be strange if you weren't attracted to her," Matt said.

"I can't do anything about it."

"I get that." Matt sat back down. "The two of you have an agreement."

They'd had an agreement. And it was a smart agreement, a marriage of convenience, each living their own lives, sharing responsibility for Eli while staying out of each other's way.

That was, until last night, until Sage tried to change the terms, until TJ realized how very badly he wanted to change the terms as well.

"TJ?" Matt prompted.

"What?"

"You zoned out."

"I'm… It's… Crap."

"What?"

TJ dropped into his chair. "She offered. Last night, she said we should have sex with each other."

Matt's eyes widened.

"And not just last night. It wasn't a heat of the moment kind of thing. She very reasonably and rationally made a case for us sleeping together on an ongoing basis."

Matt remained silent.

Now that TJ was rolling, he found he didn't want to stop. "She said we both needed a sex life. She said she didn't want to have an affair. You have to admire that. I admire that. But she said the only solution was for us to sleep together, with each other."

TJ closed and straightened the Mumbai agreement, tapping the edge sharply against the desk. "Like some kind of friends with benefits arrangement. But we're not friends with benefits. We're married to each other. And for Eli's sake, we have to stay together. If we let it get complicated, somebody's going to get hurt."

"You *turned her down*?" When Matt finally spoke, his tone was incredulous.

TJ didn't think it was an outrageous decision. He thought it was a prudent decision. It was a responsible decision. "What would you have done?"

"If my sexy, beautiful wife suggested we sleep together?"

"You know it's not that simple."

"Simple or not, I would never have insulted her by saying no."

TJ opened his mouth to counter the statement, but nothing came to his mind.

August moved along, and Sage began to think about the upcoming school year. Both Eli and Heidi were now healthy and happy. Heidi still had her sad moments, but the children were making friends and joining in on activities. Eli was playing baseball, while Heidi had decided to join a kids' art club. She loved painting, and the group spent a lot of time with their easels in the park painting landscapes.

While working on the seaside festival, Sage had grown curious about TJ's other charitable causes. He was a stalwart contributor to Highside Hospital, and she wondered if he might also consider supporting St. Bea's. Gerry Carter, the chief accountant, had given her access to part of Tide Rush Investment's accounting system, and she discovered TJ's contributions to philanthropic organizations had fallen off in recent years.

She also came across hundreds of requests that had been submitted through the company website and in letters. She'd sorted through them all, entering them into a spreadsheet that tracked organizations, dates, amounts and causes. Then she added who and what it would benefit, thinking that would be helpful information.

Now she heard the front door close, and she glanced guiltily at the time. It was nearly ten in the evening. TJ often worked late, and she tried to keep to the upstairs while he was at home. They were polite to each other, but their relationship had never really recovered from her suggestion that they sleep together.

It had been an impulsive thing to do, and she regretted it. But she knew she couldn't go any further with her philanthropic ideas without talking to him. She steeled herself and left the office, finding TJ in the kitchen.

He looked up from the refrigerator as she entered, his expression telling her he was surprised to see her.

"Hi, TJ." She moved closer, keeping the breakfast island between them.

"You're up," he said as he selected a soft drink.

"I was using the office computer." She held up a sheaf of papers as evidence.

"Thirsty?" He kept the fridge door open.

She shook her head. Then she thought better of her answer. She wanted this to be a friendly conversation. "Sure. Whatever you're having."

He filled two glasses with ice from the dispenser and split the soda between them.

"I've been looking at the philanthropic accounts," she told him.

A micro expression flicked across his face. If she had to guess, she'd say she'd annoyed him. But she was going to ignore it.

"You've received a lot of requests."

He set one of the glasses in front of her. "There are a lot of good causes."

She slid up onto a stool and put the papers on the island countertop. "I notice you've favored health and educational causes in the past."

"I suppose," he said.

"Other than Highside Hospital and Invo North College, you've mostly donated to national organizations."

His gaze flicked to the papers.

She took the opportunity to turn them to face him. "I've sorted and organized the requests."

He seemed surprised. He flipped over the first few pages. "This was a lot of work."

"There were hundreds of requests. I have some ideas, well, some recommendations on what you might want to consider supporting."

"We," he said. "What we might want to consider supporting."

She met his gaze, feeling a familiar shaft of attraction. It took her a minute to form the word. "We."

"Whatever you want," he said, setting down the report and heading for the family room.

She scrambled to follow. "I don't want to do it that way."

"I don't have time to help. There's a lot going on at the office."

"So I gathered," she said. Her tone came out as a rebuke.

He sat down on the sofa, setting the drink in front of him. "That's how I make my money."

"You don't seem very happy about it."

He glared at her for a moment.

She told herself not to be intimidated. She sat down next to him, this time putting the report on the coffee table. "I was thinking about keeping things local, or maybe statewide. There's a lot of good that can be done by focusing your contributions."

"Our contributions."

Sage sighed. "Whatever they are, they've dropped off in the past few years."

"Do whatever you want."

"I don't *want* to do whatever I want."

"Sage." Her name was a growl.

She looked at him. "What? *What?* I can't figure you out?" Her voice rose. "You don't want to sleep with me. Fine. I won't sleep with you."

The room went deadly silent.

They both breathed deeply.

He broke the silence. "You think I don't want to sleep with you?"

She didn't know how to answer that. She'd offered. He'd said no. Was there any other possible way to take that?

"I'm dying to sleep with you," he said.

She gave her head a little shake, certain she'd heard him wrong.

"You are beautiful," he said, his tone husky. His hand slowly rose, and his fingertips feathered her cheek. "You are so sexy and smart and funny."

"But…"

"I can't look at you without remembering what you offered, remembering my reaction, kicking myself for being such an idiot."

She could barely believe what she was hearing. "TJ?"

"You were right. You are right. That is… I mean… If you still feel…" His head dipped toward her, his lips grazing hers, gently at first and then with clear purpose.

Her surprise had her frozen. But then her body reacted with an avalanche of hormones. She all but fell into him, into his embrace, his name running over and over through her mind.

His forearm was firm on the small of her back, pressing her tighter against him. His spread fingers tunneled into her hair, anchoring her for a deep, passionate kiss.

She tipped her head, and her own arms wrapped around his neck. She could feel his heat, hear the hiss of his breath, smell the spice of his skin. And his kisses tasted like magic.

But she was hot and needy and restless. She reached between them and peeled off her top, revealing her white lacy bra.

He drew back, a look of awe in his expression. Then his tanned hand cupped her breast.

"Oh, Sage," he whispered.

She flipped the clasp of her bra, tossing it aside.

His gaze locked with hers, he threw off his jacket and unbuttoned his shirt.

She was past the point of no return. There was no going back. She stood and stripped off her jeans, dispensing with her panties.

A smile grew on his face. Then he sobered, shucking his own pants. Then naked, he took her back in his arms.

They were skin on skin. Their lips met and their legs entwined. Sage felt herself falling, falling into oblivion. Nothing existed but TJ.

She touched him everywhere, and he returned the favor, her face, her breasts, her thighs. His hands were deft and certain, and her body flushed and sensitized, growing dewy and heated in his wake.

She reveled in the feel of his muscles, his broad shoulders, bulging biceps, the flatness of his stomach, the strength of his thighs.

"Yes," he groaned in her ear. "That is so…"

His entire body tensed, and in a split second she was on her back, sinking into the soft cushions as his weight came down on top of her. She felt like liquid beneath him, and she parted her thighs, wrapping her legs around the heat of his body as they merged together.

As his pace increased, her arms wrapped tighter and tighter around him. Spasms of pleasure began in her toes, pulsating upward. He stroked harder, went deeper. She met him thrust for thrust, sensations intensifying.

He reached beneath her, changing their angle, and a sudden burst of sunshine lit up her brain. Her body catapulted, throbbing hard, contracting right down to her core.

"Yes! TJ, yes, yes."

"Sage," he groaned. "My beautiful, beautiful Sage."

The light in her brain subsided to a glow, first red, then purple, then calming to blue, where she bobbed and floated on joy.

"You were right," he whispered in her ear, his body a soothing weight on top of her. "You were so very right."

"Took you long enough." Matt joined TJ next to the barbecue on the patio in TJ's backyard.

"Long enough for what?"

A round of burgers and brats were sizzling on the grill. Eli and a few of his friends were climbing trees at the edge of the yard. And Sage was standing on the lawn in a white summer dress, chatting with Melissa and holding one of Caleb's twins in her arms.

TJ couldn't pull his gaze from her.

"Don't play dumb. You're staring like she's a bowl of triple caramel swirl."

"Better," TJ said without hesitation.

Matt grinned. "I knew you'd take my advice."

TJ watched Sage sway, gently patting the baby's back. "Right. Because I make all of my life decisions based on your advice."

"You should."

"It had nothing to do with you."

"I'm not saying I came up with the idea. I'm just saying I saw it first."

"Saw what first?" Caleb appeared behind them.

"That TJ was attracted to his wife."

"Who wouldn't be attracted to your wife?" Caleb asked.

Both TJ and Matt shot Caleb a look of incredulity.

"I mean mortal men," Caleb qualified. "I'm obviously not noticing."

"You better not be," TJ said, surprised by his visceral reaction.

After last night, he was feeling very protective of Sage. It was only natural, he told himself. It might not be a normal marriage, but it was a marriage. And now, well, now that they'd made love, he couldn't imagine her being with any other man. Not that he had a right to ask that of her. But she had said herself that she didn't want an affair.

Caleb clapped him on the back, nearly jolting the spatula out of TJ's hand. "Don't look so glum."

TJ suddenly remembered the burgers and quickly moved to flip them over. "I'm not glum."

Matt shot TJ a sly look.

"What was that?" Caleb asked, too quick not to pick up on it.

"Nothing," Matt said.

"That wasn't nothing."

TJ didn't want to play games with one of his closest friends. "My relationship with Sage has shifted."

Caleb looked worried. "What happened?"

"In a good way," TJ said.

Caleb's brow went up. "Seriously?"

"Seriously," Matt said. "And I did notice. And I did suggest it. Unlike you, who's been fixated on I don't know what for the past seven months."

"You try operating on sleep deprivation," Caleb said. "Wait. You're going to be doing precisely that come spring." His tone turned sarcastic. "You're gonna love it."

"I honestly can't wait," Matt said, sounding completely sincere.

Burgers rescued, TJ's attention went back to Sage. She looked so natural holding a baby. She must have looked exactly the same way holding Eli. TJ experienced an acute longing for all that he'd missed.

"I'm happy for you," Caleb said, pulling TJ back to the present.

TJ took in the expressions on both his friends' faces, and he realized where conjecture had taken them.

"It's not like that," he quickly put in, feeling a shot of guilt. "It's…different than that. We're in this thing. We're healthy adults. Neither of us wants to run around with anyone else."

"Does she know that's how it is?" Caleb asked with a frown.

"It was her idea," TJ said.

"You can't see danger signs?" Caleb asked.

"They have limited options," Matt said.

"You're in support of this?" Caleb asked Matt.

"Well, I'm not in support of any of the alternatives. Perpetual sexual frustration? Cheating? An open marriage? Can you imagine TJ standing by while Sage heads out on a date?"

"Stop!" TJ shouted. There was no way in the world Sage was going on a date.

"It may be a bit unorthodox," Matt said.

"It may be playing with fire." Caleb looked to TJ. "One of you is going to fall for the other."

"It won't be me," TJ said.

There wasn't any room in his heart. The knowledge made him sad. He realized he was sad for Sage. Because she sure deserved someone to fall head over heels for her.

"Then it's going to be her," Caleb said. "What are you going to do if she falls for you?"

"It was her idea," TJ repeated with determination.

He told himself she knew what she was proposing. She had to have known what she was proposing. As Matt pointed out, they didn't have a lot of alternatives.

TJ's gaze continued to rest on her holding the baby. He didn't want any of the alternatives. They'd made their choice, and right now he couldn't wait for everyone to leave tonight so they could be alone all over again.

Eleven

There was a skip in Sage's step as she made her way across the campus of Invo North College. She replayed making love with TJ again over and over in her mind. He was amazing, and she was content to take things moment to moment.

For now, she was enrolling in college. She'd pored over the course listings, coming to the surprising conclusion that she wanted to major in data analytics. Math had always been her strong suit, and anytime her work had involved spreadsheets and data sets, she'd been fascinated with the power of the tools.

After crossing the gorgeous campus, up a wide walkway lined with maple trees, she climbed the stairs to the admissions building. Through the glass doors, it was bustling with activity, lineups and conversations, with signs and monitors providing direction.

She found the enrollment office on a building map and set off down a hallway. The office was large, bright and seemingly well ordered. She joined a lineup being served by at least a dozen officers behind a long counter. Although most of the people in the lineup looked to be in their late teens, she was happy to see a number of twenty and thirtysomethings as well. She hadn't been sure how she'd fit in with the student population.

The lineup moved smoothly, and soon she was standing in front of an older woman in a navy blazer, a pair of reading glasses perched on her nose.

"Do you have your signed eight-twenty-four form?" the woman asked.

Sage quickly flipped through the papers in her hand, finding the right form. "Yes." She handed it over.

The woman scanned the form, then typed something into her computer.

"Did you select your courses online?"

"I was wait-listed for a couple," Sage answered. "But I wasn't planning to take a full course load, so if I don't get into everything this semester, it's fine."

"Hmm." The woman looked worried.

"Is that a problem?" Sage had read through the website. Invo North Pacific definitely offered part-time programs.

"No." She smiled at Sage. "Can you wait just a moment? I'll be right back."

"Why—"

The woman was gone before Sage could finish her sentence. Feeling uneasy, she glanced both ways along the counter. Everyone else seemed productively engaged in the enrollment process. She hoped the length of time she'd been away from high school wasn't going to trip her up. She had checked the mature student box.

Another woman, this one younger, maybe in her forties, slimmer and very professionally groomed, arrived. "Mrs. Bauer?"

The name took Sage by surprise. "It's Costas. Sage Costas."

"I'm sorry. Ms. Costas. Of course. I'm Bernadette Thorburn, college president." She reached across the counter, offering Sage her hand.

Surprised again, Sage shook the woman's hand.

"Do you have a few minutes to talk?" Bernadette asked.

"I suppose." She looked to the admissions officer who was standing to one side. "Are we finished? Is there anything else you need?" Sage had been prepared with an original copy of her high school transcripts and her credit card.

"Bernadette will be able to help you," the officer said.

Sage suddenly understood what was going on. TJ was a contributor to the college. They must feel his wife shouldn't need to stand in line.

"I'm fine enrolling this way," she hastily told them. She didn't want them to think she expected special privileges.

"There's another matter I'd like to discuss," Bernadette said. She was smiling, and her eyes were friendly. Whatever she wanted to discuss didn't look like it was going to be a problem. She pointed. "I can meet you at the end of the counter."

"Okay." Sage gathered up her paperwork.

She supposed whatever got the job done. Maybe they were going to let her into the wait-listed classes. That would be a bonus. Although she still wouldn't want to take all of them at once. The statistics class would be her first choice.

At the end of the counter, Bernadette held open a half door and showed Sage into an office overlooking the quad. The two sat down at a round table.

"Welcome to Invo North Pacific," Bernadette said.

"Thank you. I'm happy to be here. I'm looking forward to attending."

"I hope your son is doing well."

Sage wasn't sure how to react. "You know about Eli?"

"Whiskey Bay is a small community. The college draws from a much larger area, of course, from all across the country and internationally too. But we like to keep the local culture alive as much as we can. It provides a more unique experience for students. There's a lot to be said for the Pacific Northwest."

"I agree," Sage said. "I grew up in Seattle."

"And I understand you were valedictorian."

"That was almost a decade ago."

"And you've had life experience since."

Sage nodded.

"Community involvement and influence, and I heard you whipped the Seaside Festival into shape. Donations were up. Attendance was up. But expenses were down."

That characterization seemed blown out of proportion. "I didn't contribute much. Just logic and reason where it came to the budget, and I probably had more time than people have had in the past to pore over the books."

"Whatever it was, it worked. I have friends on the organizing committee, and they were impressed."

"Well, then, thank you." Sage wasn't sure what else she could or should say.

"I've been authorized to bring a proposal to you." Bernadette took a beat. "The board has advised me they'd like to nominate you as a trustee."

Sage struggled to understand the statement. "For the Seaside Festival?"

Did it even have a board? Trustees?

"A trustee for Invo North Pacific."

It took Sage a moment to find the words. "For *the college*? I'm not qualified to sit on a college board."

Bernadette gave a light laugh. "If I had a dollar for every time somebody told me that. No, let me rephrase. If I had a dollar for every time a woman told me that. Don't sell yourself short, Sage. They're not looking for a particular skill set. They want community members with life experience who understand the culture of the Pacific Northwest."

"Who can raise money." Sage was beginning to understand. "You want Mrs. Bauer."

Bernadette shook her head. "It's a whole lot more than that. You didn't just hand out a check for the festival. You inspired others to get on board with funding it. Then you managed all that money, spending it prudently. The Seaside Festival is Whiskey Bay's marquee event, and you improved it immensely, and in a very short time."

"Still…"

"Let me add this. Gender balance is an issue for Invo North Pacific, like it is for most college boards. We have less than twenty percent female trustees. I'll be blunt. We need more."

Again, Sage thought she understood. "I'll be a token woman."

Bernadette swiftly shook her head. There was a gleam of determination in her eyes. "There'll be nothing token about it. From what I've heard, you are smart, energetic and determined. I have no doubt you can make a difference. And I can promise you this. It will be a rewarding and enriching experience."

Sage found herself curious about Bernadette. "Is it hard for you? Being a woman at the head of a college?"

"You bet it's hard. But it gets easier over time. And it's important. And I am more than willing to do the work."

"You've sold me," Sage said.

It sounded challenging. It sounded meaningful. It was exactly the kind of contribution Sage wanted to make to her new community.

TJ couldn't stop staring at Sage. The flicker of a hurricane lamp on the deck at Neo reflected off her creamy skin. Her hair was up, wisps brushing over her temples, highlighted by the flash of her dangling diamond earrings that matched the pendant necklace resting against her chest.

He'd given her the jewelry last night at a rollicking at-home birthday celebration with cake and presents and singing. The children had loved it. Sage had been uncertain about accepting the jewelry. He knew she was bothered by the expense. But he wasn't bothered at all—exactly the opposite. She looked stunning in diamonds, and he was thrilled to give them to her.

The waiter had just popped open a bottle of champagne and filled their flutes. The breeze from the ocean was soft, the stars alight, the moon a thin crescent in the distance.

"Happy birthday," TJ said as he raised his glass to hers.

"I don't need two birthdays." But she was smiling as she spoke, and she accepted his toast.

"You deserve two birthdays. You deserve more than that for all the ones I missed."

She touched the necklace. "You don't have to make up for lost time."

He wanted to make up for lost time. He wanted it for Eli and, though he knew it didn't make any sense, he wanted it for Sage too. Her life had been tough while she was alone. There were a thousand ways he could have made it easier.

He wished he could spend every second of the rest of his life with them both. But that was impossible. Reality was already crowding in.

"I have to go to New York," he told her.

Her smile dimmed. "When?"

Guilt and disappointment rushed through him. "Tomorrow. It's just for a couple of days."

"Okay."

"I don't want to go."

"It's fine, TJ." She smiled again.

He still wanted to explain. "There are times when the owner of the company has to show up and sign things in person."

"That sounds important."

"They're closing a very big deal. It's a huge accomplishment for the New York office, and they'll appreciate the attention. Not to mention the client. The client will like the attention as well."

"Can you tell me about it?"

"I could. But the details would be boring. It's a Japanese-American merger of two aerospace companies."

"The space station?"

"Mars."

"You call that boring?"

"They're not actually going to Mars. Not this weekend, anyway. It's all about testing systems and innovations that might someday help with a Mars mission."

"That still doesn't qualify as boring."

"I'm just the money guy."

She touched her necklace again. "That you are."

Inspiration hit him. He leaned forward and took her hand, holding it across the table. "Come to New York with me?"

Her surprise was obvious.

"Come with me," he repeated. "We can stay at the Plaza, dine at Daniel, take in a show."

"What about the kids?"

"That's why we have two housekeepers."

"But overnight?"

"They love Kristy. They'll barely notice we're gone."

"I don't know… It seems…"

He raised her hand to his lips and gave it a gentle kiss. "Come to New York with me. We deserve a weekend to ourselves."

She gazed deep into his eyes, and he felt like time stopped.

He wanted her in New York. He suddenly realized how much he needed her in New York. Making love with her, then sleeping in separate bedrooms wasn't cutting it for him. He wanted to hold her in his arms all night long.

"Please," he whispered.

She hesitated but then gave the barest of nods.

His smile went wide. "If we weren't already drinking champagne, I'd order some."

"This is a strange life I'm leading," she said half to herself.

"Just relax and enjoy the ride." He handed her a leather-bound menu. "Now, tell me about your day?"

She opened the menu on the table. "I registered for college."

"Good for you." He waited. He knew there was more.

"Funny thing," she said, her gaze staying fixed on the menu pages.

"What's that?"

"They asked me something else."

"Oh." He kept his expression neutral.

"They asked me to serve as a trustee."

TJ immediately grinned. "I hope you said yes."

"Bernadette Thorburn was very convincing."

"Bernadette is like that."

"I'm really not sure I have enough experience."

"You're going to be fantastic." He opened his own menu, thrilled to learn she'd agreed to serve on the college board.

It was exactly what she needed to use her talents and get more involved in the community. He wanted her to like it here in Whiskey Bay. No, he wanted her to love it here.

"When are you starting?" he asked.

"Not until October."

The answer confused him. "But they said—" He quickly stopped himself.

She slowly raised her head to stare at him.

He stilled. Then he swallowed.

It took her about three seconds to figure it out. "*You* put them up to it."

He shook his head.

She clearly wasn't about to buy his denial. "You used your money and influence to get me a trustee gig?"

"It wasn't like that."

The tone of her voice rose. "Why would you do that?"

"I merely suggested they might consider you."

"You made a suggestion? Did you threaten to pull your donation?"

"Sage, stop. I only suggested. They could say yes or they could say no. And they knew that. The rest was all you."

She closed her menu. "I don't believe you."

"Have you decided already?"

"What?"

He looked pointedly at her closed menu, hoping against hope to move the conversation along.

"Yes, I have. I've decided to go home and make myself a sandwich."

"You don't want to do that."

She couldn't be that angry. It wasn't possible for her to be that angry over such a little thing.

She reached for her purse.

He touched her arm. "Don't. Stop. Look at me."

She paused, gazing at him with suspicion.

"How do you think these things work?"

"I don't really want to know how they work. And I sure don't want to be involved."

"You wanted to be involved two minutes ago."

"That's when I thought I legitimately had something to offer."

"You *do* have something to offer. You have *a lot* to offer. That's why I put your name forward, and that's why Bernadette agreed to set it up." He took a breath.

She didn't immediately bolt.

He took that as a good sign. "The way these things work is you get a little bit of influence, and then you parlay it into more influence, and so on, and so on. You did a fantastic job with the festival."

"Don't pretend this was my performance at the festival. It was your money, plain and simple."

"Partly. Yes, of course, that was a factor. But so what? That's how everybody gets in. You obviously liked what Bernadette had to say. You obviously think you can make a contribution. So make it. From this second on, I can't help you at all. The door is open, you can walk through it or not."

She glared at him in silent suspicion.

He wanted to say more, but he knew it was smarter to stop talking.

"If that's all true, why weren't you honest to begin with?" she asked. "Why weren't you up-front with me?"

He acknowledged it was a fair question. He hadn't wanted to manipulate her. He'd wanted to make her happy. He'd pictured her conversation with Bernadette over and over in his mind, and he quite simply got a kick out of thinking about her joy.

"I wanted it to make you happy," he said.

She heaved a sigh. "It did. But then it made me mad. And now I'm not happy anymore."

"I'm sorry. I didn't think it through."

"You mean you didn't think you'd get caught."

"I normally don't."

"You do this all the time?"

"No, no." He could feel himself losing ground. "Not at home. In business. Just a little bit. Sometimes the direct approach isn't the best approach. Sometimes it's better to plant a seed and then stand back and let it germinate."

"I'm not a seed."

"I know."

"I don't want to germinate."

"I understand."

"I don't want you germinating me ever—" It was obvious she struggled but then failed to stop a smile. "That didn't sound right."

"It sounded sexy." He dared to take her hand. "I won't try to manipulate you again. I promise. But as for the germinating part…"

"It's not the manipulation." She paused. "I mean, it is the manipulation. But it's more the money. You don't need to use your money to make me happy."

"I'm not." He wasn't.

She gave a sad smile. She obviously wasn't convinced. He'd have to work on that.

"You're going on an airplane?" Heidi asked in a wary voice.

Both kids were on the sofa in the family room, still in their pajamas after breakfast. Sage and TJ were in the armchairs across from them.

"Kristy will be here the whole time," Sage said, her guilt surging.

"We'll have a great time," Kristy chimed in from where she was loading the dishwasher.

"I've never *been* on an airplane," Heidi said.

"I was on a helicopter once," Eli said. "I don't remember it though." He looked to TJ. "Will you go to the Mets game?"

Sage and TJ exchanged a look. She hadn't seen this one coming.

"Are you telling me there's a Mets game tonight?" TJ asked Eli.

Eli moved up to the edge of the sofa. "It's their first home game this month."

"I like baseball," Heidi said, her expression growing hopeful.

TJ closed his eyes and his chin dropped to his chest.

"I've never seen a live major league game," Eli added.

"He's your son," Sage said to TJ, struggling not to laugh. "Dropping seeds and letting them germinate."

"Do they have ballpark franks?" Heidi asked. "Do they bring them to your seat?"

TJ raised his head. "Are you two saying you want to go to New York?"

"Yes!" both children sang out in unison.

TJ raised his hands in defeat. "Kristy?"

"Yes, boss?" Kristy moved from the kitchen into the family room.

"Would you be able to come to New York overnight?"

"You bet I can."

"Yippee!" Eli sprang to his feet on the sofa.

Heidi followed a little more slowly.

Sage felt her heart swell with joy. Seeing the kids this excited was so wonderfully ordinary.

She leaned closer to TJ. "Thank you."

He retrieved his phone from his shirt pocket. "I told you, you never have to thank me for taking care of my son." His gaze went to Heidi. "Or my daughter."

"Upstairs," Kristy said brightly to the kids, urging them down from the sofa. "We need to pack your things."

"Our flight is in an hour," TJ told her. Then he pressed a speed dial button on his phone. "I'm still getting you alone," he said to Sage.

She grinned, feeling lighthearted, happy and excited. She wanted to be alone with TJ too.

"Hi, Danica," he said to his assistant. "We're going to need a second suite at the Plaza. There'll be five passengers on the jet. And can you get us some Mets tickets. We'll need five." He paused. Then he frowned. "True. You better cancel that reservation. It sounds like we're having hot dogs at the stadium."

Sage chuckled.

"Thanks, Danica." He ended the call. "This isn't funny," he said to Sage.

"It's a little bit funny."

"Do you know how hard it is to get reservations at Daniel?"

"Poor baby." She rose and cradled his face in her hands.

"Kiss it better?" he asked hopefully.

She leaned slowly down. He closed his eyes and raised his chin.

At the last moment, she planted a kiss on his forehead instead.

"Oh, no, you don't," he said.

Before she could react, she was in his lap, pressed against his chest, his arm firmly around her shoulders.

"That's not going to cut it," he told her.

"You must be really upset," she teased.

"Devastated," he answered, and then he was kissing her mouth.

She kissed him back, her lips melding with his, softening and parting. Her arms went around his neck, and she held him tight, her emotions in a free fall. He was such an amazing man. He was a wonderful father. Their lives might be exceptionally complicated, but right now, right this minute, for today and tonight and tomorrow, she would let them be simple.

She and TJ and their children were taking a short vacation, just like families did all over the country. Well, most families likely piled in the minivan and drove down the highway to a seaside motel. But a private jet and the Plaza were almost the same thing...almost.

"What is it?" TJ drew back and took in her expression.

It was hard for her to put into words. Instead, she made a joke. "Like I said before, this is a strange life I'm leading."

"It's a perfectly normal life."

"I feel like an impostor." There. That was closer.

It took him a second to answer. "The last thing you are is an impostor. You're my wife. You're the mother of my son."

His words warmed her, and she let herself lean into his strength.

He smoothed his palm over the back of her hair. "Like *I* said before, relax and enjoy the ride."

"I will. I am." It was the only thing that made sense. And it was what she wanted, anyway.

She touched his face, smoothing her fingertips along the curve of his cheek and the jut of his jaw. Then she kissed him again.

The children's voices echoed down the stairs, and she knew they had only moments alone, but she kissed him deep and long, falling into the moment and into the fantasy she intended to perpetuate for the next two days.

Twelve

By the time the game had ended, both kids had been asleep on their feet. Kristy had taken them into the suite across the hall, promising them bubble baths in the oversize tub and a story once they were tucked in. TJ was finally alone with Sage.

Theirs was a two-bedroom suite, but he had no intention of using the second bedroom.

"I have room service coming," he told her as she kicked off her runners.

"Hot dogs and malted milk balls weren't enough for you?"

"They weren't exactly what I had in mind when I planned this."

She was smiling as she made her way into the living room. "But it was fun."

"It was fun," he agreed, peeling the heavy foil from

the top of the bottle of Cabernet Sauvignon that was waiting for them on the bar.

The game, in fact the whole day, had been more fun than he'd expected. They'd gone to the zoo, where Heidi had fallen in love with the cats. TJ had bought her a stuffed snow leopard, while Eli had chosen a rubber snake. Both Heidi and Sage had shuddered when Eli draped the python around his neck. TJ was gaining a whole new appreciation for the differences between boys and girls.

"Thirsty?" he asked Sage, sliding two red wine goblets out of the overhanging rack.

"Is that a thirst-quenching red?" she asked, coming up behind him.

"It will complement the charcuterie board that's on its way up. I'm chilling champagne to go with the chocolate strawberries."

"Are you planning to get drunk?"

"We don't have to drink it all." He started to pour.

She glanced around the room. "Does this seem normal to you?"

"Does what seem normal?"

"This room. The wine. The strawberries."

"I haven't had this vintage before." He glanced at the label. "But Caleb highly recommended it."

"You consulted with Caleb on the wine?"

"Before we left Whiskey Bay. I didn't call him between innings or anything." TJ offered her one of the glasses.

"Because that would be odd?" She accepted the glass.

"I called him last night, after you agreed to come along."

"Before Eli and Heidi decided to crash."

"The night is still young." TJ raised his glass and waited for Sage to take a sip.

Strangely, although he was more than glad to be alone with her now, he didn't begrudge having the kids and Kristy along for the day. It had been fun. It had been great. As a package, the day had been perfect.

"Do you like it?" he asked Sage.

"It's delicious."

TJ took a taste. It was everything Caleb had promised.

There was a knock at the door.

The waiter entered with a rolling cart and took a few minutes to set up the table that was positioned in a turret of windows overlooking the park.

TJ saw the waiter to the door and gave him a tip. When he turned back, Sage was biting into a chocolate-dipped strawberry.

"Those are supposed to go with the champagne," he said, making his way toward her.

She grinned unrepentantly. "I'm a maverick."

"The tastes will clash." He wanted her to have the best possible culinary experience.

A gleam in her eyes, she took another swallow of her wine. "It all tastes good to me."

"Bohemian."

"Snob."

She was clearly teasing, but the accusation hit its mark anyway.

"You think so?" he asked, suddenly worried he'd overdone the evening.

"Oh, I do think so, Mr. Phone-a-Wine-Consultant."

"It wasn't the most expensive bottle in the cellar."

She took another sip, then wrinkled her nose. "Cutting corners, are we?"

He waltzed forward and swung an arm around her waist. "I can't win with you, can I?"

"Oh, I wouldn't say that." She went soft and supple against him, and a sensual glow came up deep in her jade-colored eyes.

"I take it back."

"Oh, you will." She moved to disentangle herself.

"What? What are you doing?"

She took a step away from him.

"Where are you going?" he asked.

"To change."

"Please don't change." Even as he made the joke, he realized he didn't want her to change. He didn't want to change a single thing about her.

"I took your advice," she said.

He moved toward her, but she backed off some more.

"Clearly, I'm giving you very bad advice."

"I'm going to change my clothes, TJ. I took your credit card."

"*Your* credit card."

"And bought a little outfit."

He stilled. His mouth went dry. "Define *little*."

She gave him a saucy grin. "I think you'll like it."

"Then what are you waiting for?"

"You don't want to finish the snacks?"

"The snacks will wait." He couldn't. He couldn't wait to see what kind of an outfit she'd bought.

"I wouldn't want to compromise your culinary experience."

"You can compromise anything you want."

She laughed at that. Then she turned for the bedroom, sauntering through the door and closing it behind her.

TJ took a deep breath, telling himself to stay cool.

He moved to an armchair and sat down, taking a swallow of the wine.

Whatever she looked like when she walked back through the door, he absolutely was not going to rush things. He'd take his time, just like he'd planned. He'd make it romantic, just like he'd planned. They had all night to—

She appeared in the doorway, and he nearly dropped his glass.

She was draped in purple satin—a short spaghetti-strapped nightie with flat lace panels along the neck and hem. Her shoulders were smooth and slender, hair copper under the soft lights. Her thighs were shapely, her calves sleek, and her feet were bare. Her auburn hair billowed around her face, bouncing to her collarbone and framing her slim neck.

He abandoned his wine, rolling to his feet, stripping off his polo shirt as he crossed the floor.

"What do you think?" she asked a bit breathlessly.

"Huh?" He had to shake himself out of a daze.

"Do you like it?" She spread her arms and did a pirouette.

By the time she'd turned, he had her in his arms. "I love it."

"You've barely seen it."

"I'll see it more later." He kissed her, bending her backward, going deep, drinking in the taste of her.

She held on to his shoulders, and he wrapped an arm around her, stabilizing her, using his free hand to roam the satin of her breathtaking outfit, smoothing his palm over her stomach, her breasts, her rear. Every inch of her felt fantastic.

Her breathing rate increased, her chest rising and

falling. She kissed him with fervor, thrusting her tongue to parry with his. Her lips were so sweet. Her thighs were sleek and firm. And her breasts were soft beneath his hand, her nipples peaking against his touch.

She arched her back, and a soft moan came from her lips.

Desire flashed through him, and he scooped her into his arms, carrying her back into the bedroom, laying her on the four-poster bed, atop the crisp sheets, the moonlight filtering through sheer curtains to dance on the sheen of her skin.

He shucked his pants to lie down beside her, peeling the spaghetti strap from her shoulder, kissing his way to her breast, drawing her nipple into his mouth.

Her hands buried themselves in his short hair. She moaned again, gently flexing beneath him.

The silk bunched up at her waist. He drew back to stare at the sensual picture she made against the stark sheets, arms above her head, one knee bent.

"You are beautiful," he whispered, brushing the back of his hand from her elbow to the side of her breast, then farther down to the nip of her waist and the curve of her hip. Her eyes were buffed jade, her hair a dark halo.

His touch followed her hip bone to her navel and below, dipping farther and farther.

She closed her eyes, and her thighs twitched open.

He dipped into her heat, his pulse pounding, his breathing labored.

When he couldn't stand it anymore, he stripped off his boxers and covered her with his body.

She wrapped herself around him, kissing his mouth, her fingers kneading the muscles of his back. When her heat and softness engulfed him, he groaned her name, balling his fists, searching for strength.

He was determined to take it slow. She deserved romance. She deserved to be cherished. She deserved to be the only woman in his world. Just for tonight, he told himself. Just for tonight, he'd banish everything from his mind, everything but Sage.

He drew his head back, just far enough to focus on her. Her eyes were closed. Her lips were deep red. Her cheeks were flushed.

She moved with him, their rhythm easy, their bodies in sync. Pleasure ebbed through him, pulsing, growing, taking over his body and his mind. His pace increased, and her hold tightened. Before he knew it, he was out of control, moving faster, reaching higher, holding, holding, holding back every second that he could until a world of color, heat and light exploded behind his eyes and his muscles convulsed with release.

"Sage!" Her name was wrenched from his lips, then it thundered over and over inside his brain.

It was midmorning, and the house was completely quiet. Sage stood in the opening between the living room and the family room and drank in the stillness.

Eli and Heidi were at their first full day of school. Whiskey Bay Elementary was a fifteen-minute bus ride away, and they'd been thrilled to hop on the school bus at the end of the driveway. TJ had gone to the office, and Kristy was back at college. Verena wasn't due for at least an hour.

Sage tried to remember how long it had been since she'd been completely alone.

There was course reading waiting for her in the office,

and two reports from the college board. Plus, there were always the philanthropic requests for Tide Rush Investments. Although she had that part down to a system, it was always satisfying to find a new project that fit their criteria.

But for now, just for a few minutes, she wanted to savor the peace.

Maybe some tea—since she'd learned how to use the cappuccino machine, a latte was her beverage of choice in the morning. But today didn't feel like a latte day. It felt like herbal tea, maybe something with lemon.

The family room wasn't messy, but it was comfortably disheveled. She liked that.

On the way past the table, she closed Heidi's coloring book and put the stray pencils into the case. Eli's rubber snake was coiled up on one of the chairs. It had stopped startling Sage a few days ago. TJ's plaid shirt was draped over the back of a chair.

She reached out and touched the shirt. He'd been wearing it yesterday playing catch in the backyard with Eli. He'd stripped down to his T-shirt before dinner, because the sun was hitting the deck, and it was hot in front of the barbecue.

They'd grilled burgers and eaten ice cream. Yesterday had come close to being perfect.

Sage lifted the shirt and pressed the soft fabric to her face. She inhaled the subtle scent of TJ, emotions rushing through her. TJ himself was close to perfect.

Maybe he was perfect.

He was perfect for her.

"Hello?" Melissa's voice called out from the front foyer.

Sage lowered the shirt from her face to call back. "I'm in the family room."

She was getting used to the casual drop-in culture of the four oceanfront houses. She couldn't quite bring herself to walk into anyone else's house yet. But she was getting there.

"Kids get off all right?" Melissa asked.

"They couldn't wait to leave."

"That's the spirit."

"We'll see if the novelty lasts." It was a lot to hope that they'd love school every morning all year long.

"I didn't mind school," Melissa said, her glance going to the shirt in Sage's hand.

"Laundry," Sage said, hooking the shirt over the back of one chair, wondering why she felt flustered. "I was about to make tea."

"Love some."

Sage headed for the kitchen, and Melissa followed.

"When do your classes start?" Melissa asked.

"Thursday. I decided to just stick with the two. I don't want to shortchange the philanthropic work for Tide Rush. There are a lot of requests coming in."

"Free money is popular. Who could have guessed?"

Sage gave an eye roll to Melissa's sarcasm as she began filling the kettle.

Melissa laughed. "I say that as the person who asked you first."

"That's true. You did. Do you need a contribution for next year?"

"Not yet. I'll hit you up in the spring."

"I'll be here." As she spoke, Sage realized her future looked bright.

Her future with TJ felt good. Maybe it felt too good.

She found herself glancing at his shirt again. Before Melissa interrupted, Sage had been cuddling his shirt, smiling and musing on his perfection.

That couldn't be good.

"Sage?" Melissa asked.

"Hmm?"

"The kettle's overflowing."

Sage glanced down. "Oops." She quickly shut off the tap.

"Is something wrong?"

"No. Nothing's wrong."

Melissa moved up beside her at the sink, concern in her tone. "Is it TJ? Are there…problems?"

Melissa knew about their unorthodox sex life. It had been her idea in the first place.

"It's good," Sage assured her. "Really good."

Melissa's gaze sharpened. "Too good."

Sage opened her mouth to lie but then changed her mind. "He's… Yeah. Maybe too good is the right way to describe it. He's so incredible. He's great with the kids. Eli adores him. He's patient and gentle with Heidi. She's gaining confidence by the day."

"And with you?"

Sage paused. "He's off the charts. In every way you can imagine. I… We…"

Melissa's arm went around Sage's shoulders. "You're in love with him."

Sage closed her eyes, anxiety and relief washing through her in equal measures. "I can't believe I let it happen."

"Do you know how he feels?"

"He seems happy. He's attentive. He's relaxed. Our

conversations are fun and funny. He trusts me with his money. Our sex life is terrific."

"Are you going to tell him?"

Sage immediately shook her head. She backed away from Melissa, holding up her palms. "No. Oh, no, no. That wasn't part of the deal."

"The deal can change."

"Not this deal. We're co-parenting."

"And you're living together. And you're sleeping together. And you're sharing a bank account. That sounds a whole lot like marriage to me."

"The marriage part isn't the problem." Sage stepped back and removed the kettle from the sink, drying it off with a towel before setting it on the stove.

"I've seen the way he looks at you," Melissa said.

"That's lust." Sage knew TJ desired her.

"I bet it's something more."

"You can't read his mind." Sage set the burner to high.

"I can see love in his eyes."

Sage swallowed. She wanted to hope, but she didn't dare. "It's not going to end that way."

"You have no idea how it's going to end."

"Lauren," she said simply.

"People get over their losses. They move on."

"Do you think?" Sage turned to look Melissa in the eyes. She wanted to hope. She very desperately wanted to hope that TJ could love her. "Do you actually think it's possible?"

"I do think it's possible. I think it's likely."

"I don't know…"

"Just consider telling him," Melissa said while the kettle began to boil.

Sage nodded.

She did think about telling him. It circled through her mind through their tea and conversation. What would happen if she told TJ she loved him? She pictured him looking confused. Then she pictured him looking horrified. Then she pictured him looking delighted. She let her fantasy TJ say he loved her back.

He smiled. He hugged her close. He kissed her and told her he loved her more than anything else in the world.

The image was so compelling, that by the time Melissa left, Sage was ready to take the risk.

She held his shirt in her arms, hugging it to her chest, inhaling the scent again. Then she laughed at herself. She wasn't going to spend the rest of the day mooning around the house like a lovesick calf.

Gripping the shirt, she marched down the hall to TJ's bedroom. The door was open, as it generally was, but she found herself hesitating in the doorway.

She'd never gone into TJ's room. They didn't sleep together. Sage stayed upstairs with the children, and TJ slept in his own bed.

At first, she'd respected his privacy, and then it had become habit. There was little reason for her to come down to this end of the hall.

Now she took a step inside.

His bed was perfectly made, even though Verena wasn't here yet—interesting. The curtains were closed over two windows on either side of the bed. The en suite door was open, and she could see a laundry hamper inside. She looked down at the shirt, laughing at herself for wanting to preserve his smell.

On the way past, she pulled the curtains open. Then she dropped the shirt in the hamper.

When she turned in the bathroom, her gaze caught on a small crystal bottle that sat on the counter. It looked like perfume.

Her heart stilled and her breathing stopped. Next to the bottle was a container of scented soap, and a glass jar of makeup pads, pink bath salts and three copper-colored candles. It was as if Lauren had just stepped out and was coming back any minute.

Sage backed out of the bathroom. As she went to leave the bedroom, she caught a glimpse of TJ's dresser. The top was covered in photos of Lauren, everything from a formal wedding shot to a picnic in the park where they were laughing and embracing on a blanket. And in the center of it all was a set of glass jewelry boxes.

Foreboding drew her forward. There were three boxes in the set, and the biggest one had Lauren's name etched on the top. The smallest held rings—a diamond engagement ring, a woman's band and a man's band beside it. Everything inside Sage turned to ice.

"What are you doing?" It was TJ's voice.

Sage whirled. She had no idea what to say. Maybe she should feel guilty. But instead she felt angry and betrayed. And intensely sad.

"Do you still have her clothes?" she asked.

TJ's jaw went lax.

"This is practically a shrine. Have you kept everything that was hers?"

"That—" his tone was rock-hard "—is none of your business."

"I'm your *wife*."

He seemed to stumble for a split second. "It's not the same thing."

Her brain reeled from the hurt and disappointment. "You mean I'm not a *real* wife."

"I was honest with you from the start."

Her heart split in two. "In other words, I'm right."

He'd acted like he cared for her. Everything he said and did made her feel like she mattered, like she was more than just Eli's mother.

"Right about what?" he asked, looking confused.

"Not right. Wrong." She made for the door.

He didn't step aside. "Wrong about what?"

She swept her arm across the room. "About this. About you. About us. I thought I could do this, TJ."

"We *are* doing this."

"No." It was crystal clear to her. "*You're* doing this. I'm doing something else altogether."

"You're not making sense."

She squeaked past him. "I have to go."

"Go where? Why? What?"

She didn't answer but kept walking.

"I never pretended I was over her," he called out.

He was right. He hadn't pretended he was over Lauren. His progress was all in Sage's mind.

"Tell me you're exaggerating," Matt said.

"Tell me you're not that stupid," Caleb said.

Afternoon sun rays bounced off the smooth water beyond the marina's rooftop patio.

"I was completely up-front with her," TJ defended. "She's known all along this was about Eli."

"You're *sleeping* with her," Matt said on a high-pitched note.

"It was *her* idea."

"People can get emotional about that sort of thing," Caleb said.

"Are you saying I should stop sleeping with her?"

TJ didn't want to do that. He truly didn't want to give that up. It was one of the few things that kept him sane. Those moments in Sage's arms, he was whole, complete. He wasn't lonely anymore.

"I'm saying you should stop lying to her," Matt said.

"I'm not lying to her." Had TJ's friends not been listening? "I've been excruciatingly honest. From minute one, I've held up my end of the deal."

"You mean the money," Matt said.

"Sure, I mean the money. Not that I can get her to spend much of it. Well, except on other people. I got her to buy a car and a few clothes. Melissa had to twist her arm to get her to buy furniture."

"It's only money," Caleb said.

"That's what *I* keep telling her."

"I mean, she doesn't only need money."

"She definitely needed money."

"You're more than generous with your money," Matt said.

TJ would have liked to take credit for that. He needed some points in this conversation. But money was easy. It was easy to make, and it was easy to give up.

Caleb leaned forward in his chair. "Eli needed more than your money. All the money in the world wouldn't have saved him without you. And Sage needs more than just your money."

"Sage isn't sick."

Caleb winced. "She needs your love."

A pain shot through TJ's head. It was as if his friends had never even met him. "I love Lauren."

"Lauren is gone," Matt said.

"Just because she's gone doesn't mean I've stopped loving her."

"Maybe not," Caleb conceded. "But it also doesn't mean you can't love Sage."

"I don't love Sage." TJ stopped himself. That sounded harsh. "I mean, I'm not in love with Sage. I love her. In a way. I guess." He suddenly felt disloyal to Lauren. "I'll never love anyone the way I loved Lauren."

Matt's tone went low, sympathetic, understanding. "Nobody is suggesting you forget Lauren. But Sage is here. She's real, and she's in your life. You can go forward, or you can go backward. But you can't do both."

"Do you want to lose Sage?" Caleb asked.

"No." TJ's answer was instantaneous.

"Do you want to hurt her?"

"No." TJ didn't want to hurt Sage.

He'd been trying his utmost not to hurt her since they'd reconnected. He owed her. What was more, he liked and respected her. He was attracted to her. He loved her.

He suddenly pictured the hurt in her eyes as she stared at his wedding picture, his wedding rings, his world with Lauren. He felt a brick hit him in the side of the head.

He'd let Lauren hurt Sage.

How could he have done that?

Lauren was forever his past. But Sage… Sage… Sage was here, and she was his future. She was warm and loving and…

He raised his chin to look at his friends, regret washing through him. "Oh, no."

"He's got it," Caleb said.

"I think he's got it," Matt echoed.

"I'm in love with Sage," TJ said. "I have to apologize."

"Not with words," Caleb said.

"Not with money," Matt said.

TJ understood. He rose. "I have to show her that there's room in my life for her."

"He's not as stupid as he looks," Matt said with a chuckle.

"Thank goodness for that," Caleb deadpanned.

TJ gave them a crooked smile, grateful as always for their blunt honesty—no matter how painful it sometimes felt.

He left the marina, striding up the pathway to his house. Sage was still gone, but he'd expected that. He was even glad. He had some work to do before they talked.

It was a good bet that she'd be back when the kids got home from school, which gave him a couple of hours. He pulled some packing boxes out of the basement and took them to his room.

He started with the easy stuff, Lauren's soap and perfume, and the clothes that were in the dresser drawers. As the items piled up, his chest grew lighter. There were hundreds of happy memories in her possessions. But that was all they were now, happy memories.

By the time he removed the last picture from the dresser, the daylight was fading through the windows. He checked his watch. Sage hadn't come home, and neither had the children.

A block of fear settled into his stomach. Where were they? Had she taken them? What if he was already too late?

Thirteen

Sage had been halfway to Seattle, her phone switched off and the kids buckled into the back seat when she'd realized she couldn't do it. She couldn't run off without a word to TJ. It was a cowardly thing to do, and it was just plain wrong to yank the kids out of school.

Sure, she was hurt. She was humiliated. But TJ was the one sticking to the terms of their agreement. She was the one who'd decided she wanted more. He was right when he said he'd been honest with her all along. He had.

She'd turned around at a rest stop and headed back home.

When she'd arrived, both kids were asleep. TJ had rushed out the front door. When he saw the sleeping children, he'd pressed his lips tight in silence and lifted Eli into his arms.

Sage carted Heidi up to her room. The little girl had

barely stirred while Sage slipped her into a nightgown and tucked her into bed.

Then Sage had steeled herself to make an apology. The best thing for everyone was to get back to an even keel. For Eli's and Heidi's sakes, she'd bury her feelings for TJ.

She'd have to stop sleeping with him. She couldn't do friends with benefits, certainly not with TJ. It would be heartbreaking to hold him in her arms and know his love was still with Lauren. She couldn't bring herself to do that.

But she could do everything else. And she would.

She made her way downstairs. It took a few minutes to find him sitting on the deck outside the family room. Her stomach fluttered, and her heart pounded in trepidation, but she forced herself forward.

"Hi," she said in a tentative voice, coming out on the deck.

He looked up quickly, as if she'd startled him.

He seemed to take in her appearance.

"I'm sorry," she said, perching on the edge of the chair next to his, gripping the armrests to steady herself. "I shouldn't have left like that."

"I tried to call," he said.

"My phone was off."

He gave a nod.

She pressed forward. "You were right. I overreacted. I mean, I reacted. I mean, I shouldn't have been surprised—"

"I didn't think you were coming back." His expression was grim.

"Like I said, I overreacted. I just needed some time, a few miles I guess, to get my head on straight." She sat up. "We had a deal, TJ. I'm prepared to honor it."

He gave a ghost of a self-deprecating smile. "To be my wife?"

"Yes. And Eli and Heidi's mother. It's better if we're together, no matter..." She cleared her throat. "It's better that we stay together."

Unexpectedly, he reached out and took her hand, stroking his thumb across her knuckles.

She wanted to snatch it away. It was just too painful to have him touch her.

"I can't—" Her voice cracked. And then all she could manage was a whisper. "I don't think we should keep sleeping together."

His thumb stilled.

"That was a mistake." She forced herself to rush on. "I know it was my idea, but it was a mistake to think it wouldn't get too complicated."

She fell to silence, and the waves below echoed in the night.

"I thought your logic was impeccable," he said.

She had too, at the time. But that was before she let her heart get in the way. She'd risked her heart, and she'd lost her heart. She was numb now, but she knew she had some very painful days ahead while she tried to get over her feelings for TJ.

"Can I show you something?" he asked.

The question took her by surprise. "Uh, sure. What is it?"

He came to his feet, centering his hold on her hand. "This way."

"Are we leaving? Is Kristy here?"

"Kristy's not here. And we're not leaving." He led her across the family room and the living room to the hallway and started down.

She stopped dead. "TJ, no. I can't."

There was no way she could go back into his bedroom.

"It'll be okay. I promise."

She shook her head, trying to pull her hand from his. "It won't be okay."

He turned to face her. "Sage." He brushed her cheek. "Trust me. I'm not going to hurt you again."

"You didn't—"

He cocked his head with an expression of disbelief.

"It was my fault, not yours," she said.

"No. It was my fault. Let me make it up to you."

Sage swallowed against the lump in her throat. Embarrassingly, tears tingled behind her eyes. "I can't go in there."

"She's gone, Sage."

His words didn't make any sense. Sage needed to flee. She needed to get away from all this.

"Lauren is gone," he said. "She's gone from my room, and she's gone from my heart." He gave a tiny smile. "From most of my heart. I'll always love what she and I had, but it's in the past. Come and see."

Emotion swelled in Sage's chest, making everything ache. How was she ever going to stop loving him?

He took her hands, backing up, drawing her down the hall with him. "You are my present, Sage."

The light was on, and she saw the cleared room, blinking to take in the enormity of it. "TJ, you didn't have to…"

"And you are my future. If you'll have me. I love you, Sage."

Her gaze darted to his. She couldn't believe she'd heard right. "You what?"

He smiled. "I love you so much. If we weren't already married, I'd be proposing right now. I never, ever, not in a million years thought I could feel this way. Stay with me." He pointed to the bedroom. "Stay here with me, every night, all the time. Let's make it real. Let's have some babies. Let's fill this house with love and laughter." He paused. "That is, if you want to. I mean, if you…"

"Love you?" she asked, feeling the brightest of joy take over her world. "I love you, TJ. I didn't mean to, but I fell very, very hard in love with you."

He wrapped his arms around her, lifting her from the floor. "I should have known."

"That I loved you?"

"That I loved you. When I saw you holding Caleb's daughter, you looked perfect. I wanted our own baby, another baby."

"More babies," she mused.

"Would you be okay with that?"

"Mommy?" came a little voice behind her.

Sage turned to see Heidi. It was the first time Heidi had called her that.

"Yes, sweetheart?" Sage let go of TJ and dropped to one knee.

"I had a bad dream."

"I'm so sorry, sweetie."

TJ crouched to join them. "Would you like Daddy to come upstairs and read you a story?"

Heidi nodded.

"Okay, pumpkin." TJ lifted Heidi into his arms.

Then he took Sage's hand.

She leaned her cheek against his shoulder as they walked. "You're the best daddy in the entire world."

Heidi's arms tightened around his neck. "Best daddy," she murmured.

"I love you both," TJ said. "I love you all."

* * * * *

If you loved this story,
pick up these other sexy and emotional reads
from New York Times *bestselling author*
Barbara Dunlop!

ONE BABY, TWO SECRETS
THE MISSING HEIR
SEX, LIES AND THE CEO

And don't miss the first two
WHISKEY BAY BRIDES *stories*

FROM TEMPTATION TO TWINS
TWELVE NIGHTS OF TEMPTATION

Available now from Harlequin Desire!

***

If you're on Twitter, tell us what you think
of Harlequin Desire! #harlequindesire

COMING NEXT MONTH FROM

HARLEQUIN *Desire*

Available March 6, 2018

#2575 MARRIED FOR HIS HEIR
Billionaires and Babies • by Sara Orwig
Reclusive rancher Nick is shocked to learn he's a father to an orphaned baby girl! Teacher Talia loves the baby as her own. So Nick proposes they marry for the baby—with no hearts involved. But he's about to learn a lesson about love...

#2576 A CONVENIENT TEXAS WEDDING
Texas Cattleman's Club: The Impostor
by Sheri WhiteFeather
A Texas millionaire must change his playboy image or lose everything he's worked for. An innocent Irish miss needs a green card immediately after her ex's betrayal. The rule for their marriage of convenience: don't fall in love. For these two opposites, rules are made to be broken...

#2577 THE DOUBLE DEAL
Alaskan Oil Barons • by Catherine Mann
Wild child Naomi Steele chose to get pregnant with twins, and she'll do anything to earn a stake for them in her family's oil business. Even if that means confronting an isolated scientist in a blizzard. But the man is sexier than sin and the snowstorm is moving in... Dare she mix business with pleasure?

#2578 LONE STAR LOVERS
Dallas Billionaires Club • by Jessica Lemmon
PR consultant Penelope Brand vowed to never, ever get involved with a client again. But then her latest client turns out to be her irresistible one-night stand, and he introduces her as his fiancée. Now she's playing couple, giving in to temptation...and expecting the billionaire's baby.

#2579 TAMING THE BILLIONAIRE BEAST
Savannah Sisters • by Dani Wade
When she arrives on a remote Southern island to become temporary housekeeper at a legendary mansion, Willow Harden finds a beastly billionaire boss in reclusive Tate Kingston. But he's also the most tempting man she's ever met. Will she fall prey to his seduction...or to the curse of Sabatini House?

#2580 SAVANNAH'S SECRETS
The Bourbon Brothers • by Reese Ryan
Savannah Carlisle infiltrated a Tennessee bourbon empire for revenge, *not* to fall for the seductive heir of it all. But as the potential for scandal builds and one *little* secret exposes everything, will it cost her the love of a man she was raised to hate?

Get 2 Free Books,

HARLEQUIN *Desire*

Plus 2 Free Gifts —

just for trying the Reader Service!

⑪HARLEQUIN® *Desire*

PR consultant Penelope Brand vowed to never, ever get involved with a client again. But then her latest client turns out to also be her irresistible one-night stand, and he introduces her as his fiancée.

Now she's playing couple, giving in to temptation…and might soon be expecting the billionaire's baby…

Read on for a sneak peek at
LONE STAR LOVERS
by Jessica Lemmon, the first book in the
***DALLAS BILLIONAIRES CLUB** trilogy!*

"You'll get to meet my brother tonight."

Penelope was embarrassed she didn't know a thing about another Ferguson sibling. She'd only been in Texas for a year, and between juggling her new business, moving into her apartment and handling crises for the Dallas elite, she hadn't climbed the Ferguson family tree any higher than Chase and Stefanie.

"Perfect timing," Chase said, his eyes going over her shoulder to welcome a new arrival.

"Hey, hey, big brother."

Now, that…that was a drawl.

The back of her neck prickled. She recognized the voice instantly. It sent warmth pooling in her belly and lower. It stood her nipples on end. The Texas accent over her shoulder was a tad thicker than Chase's, but not as lazy as it'd been two weeks ago. Not like it was when she'd invited him home and he'd leaned close, his lips brushing the shell of her ear.

Lead the way, gorgeous.

Squaring her shoulders, Pen prayed Zach had the shortest memory ever, and turned to make his acquaintance.

Correction: reacquaintance.

She was floored by broad shoulders outlined by a sharp black tux, longish dark blond hair smoothed away from his handsome face and the greenest eyes she'd ever seen. Zach had been gorgeous the first time she'd laid eyes on him, but his current look suited the air of control and power swirling around him.

A primal, hidden part of her wanted to lean into his solid form and rest in his capable, strong arms again. As tempting as reaching out to him was, she wouldn't. She'd had her night with him. She was in the process of assembling a firm bedrock for her fragile, rebuilt business and she refused to let her world fall apart because of a sexy man with a dimple.

A dimple that was notably missing since he was gaping at her with shock. His poker face needed work.

"I'll be damned," Zach muttered. "I didn't expect to see you here."

"That makes two of us," Pen said, and then she polished off half her champagne in one long drink.

Don't miss
LONE STAR LOVERS
by Jessica Lemmon, the first book in the
DALLAS BILLIONAIRES CLUB *trilogy!*

Available March 2018 wherever
Harlequin® Desire books and ebooks are sold.

www.Harlequin.com

LOVE
Harlequin
romance?

Join our Harlequin community to share your thoughts and connect with other romance readers!

Be the first to find out about promotions, news, and exclusive content!

Sign up for the Harlequin e-newsletter and download a free book from any series at

www.TryHarlequin.com

CONNECT WITH US AT:

Harlequin.com/Community

 Facebook.com/HarlequinBooks

 Twitter.com/HarlequinBooks

 Instagram.com/HarlequinBooks

 Pinterest.com/HarlequinBooks

ReaderService.com

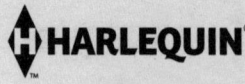

**ROMANCE WHEN
YOU NEED IT**

HSOCIAL2017